THE TIGER DRUMS

Another book for Leslie & Scoop, our good friends & artists.

BARBARA WINTHER

Barbara Winther
Oct, 10, 2013

OLD BEAR PUBLISHING

BOOKS BY BARBARA WINTHER
The Leopard Sings
The Jaguar Dances
Let It Go, Louie—Croatian Immigrants on Puget Sound
They Like Noble Causes
Hopitu
Plays from Hispanic Tales
Plays from Asian Tales
Plays from African Tales
Plays from Folktales of Africa and Asia

Copyright © 2012 Barbara Winther
All rights reserved.

ISBN: 1478330112
ISBN-13: 9781478330110

Map of Japan by Joan Kinsman
Back cover photograph by Grant Winther

*Dedicated to
my husband Grant,
who always believed
my stories
to be true*

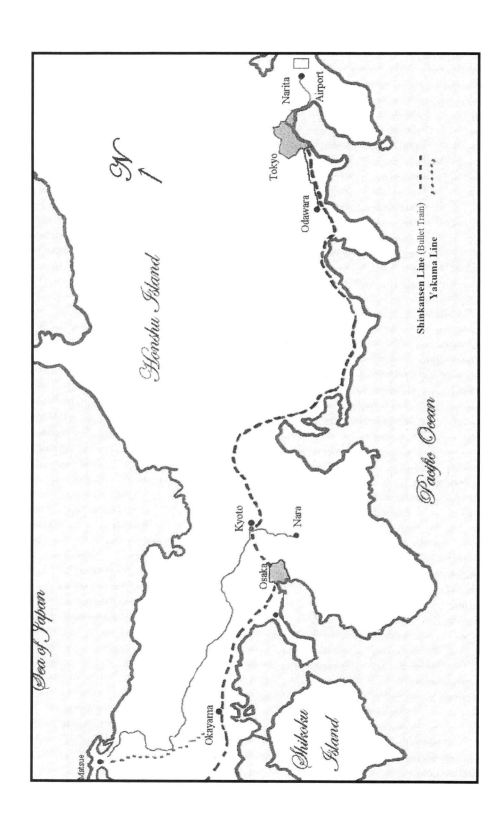

TABLE OF CONTENTS

CHAPTER 1 .... *1*
CHAPTER 2 .... *5*
CHAPTER 3 .... *11*
CHAPTER 4 .... *17*
CHAPTER 5 .... *25*
CHAPTER 6 .... *31*
CHAPTER 7 .... *37*
CHAPTER 8 .... *45*
CHAPTER 9 .... *49*
CHAPTER 10 .... *55*
CHAPTER 11 .... *61*
CHAPTER 12 .... *67*
CHAPTER 13 .... *71*
CHAPTER 14 .... *77*
CHAPTER 15 .... *83*
CHAPTER 16 .... *91*
CHAPTER 17 .... *99*
CHAPTER 18 .... *105*
CHAPTER 19 .... *111*
CHAPTER 20 .... *115*
CHAPTER 21 .... *121*
CHAPTER 22 .... *129*
CHAPTER 23 .... *137*
CHAPTER 24 .... *143*
CHAPTER 25 .... *151*
CHAPTER 26 .... *157*
CHAPTER 27 .... *165*
CHAPTER 28 .... *171*
CHAPTER 29 .... *179*
CHAPTER 30 .... *185*

CHAPTER 31 193
CHAPTER 32 201
CHAPTER 33 205
THE FAMILY TREE 209
ACKNOWLEDGMENTS 211

CHAPTER 1

The Thompson trial was only two weeks away. This was not the time to fly to Japan but in his usual charming manner Eric had convinced her to go. "Chelsea, honey, you're always so well organized. You'll be gone less than a week. It's a challenge you shouldn't refuse."

Maybe. Maybe not. What did Eric know about law? He ran a travel company. She was a full partner at McCloskey, Warner & Jarvis.

Chelsea straightened her soft felt bowler. The man across the aisle turned to stare. The hat was her talisman—jet black, gold initials CJ pinned to the brim—kept on in tense situations and always worn in the courtroom. The rolled brim and elevated dome appeared part of her unruly bangs, while the rest of her hair fell neatly just below her ears, a combination that along with her height of six feet in heels often brought double-takes. The kimonoed flight attendant had suggested placing the hat in an overhead bin. "No thanks," she had replied. "I prefer to wear it."

She leaned back into the luxurious cushion, stretched her legs under the seat in front and held the pose a moment before jerking up like a chastised child. All wrong—the place, the time, her approach. She was used to fighting for benefits. "First Class," Eric had said when he handed her the ticket, "because I'm swamped at Oriental Tours and you're saving me time and trouble."

Odd Eric had insisted she fly to Japan immediately. And alone.

Opening her black leather briefcase, she slipped out her reading glasses and the Hayashi contract. She thrust on the glasses in the authoritative way that disconcerted defense attorneys, and began studying the document page by page. Well-written, she concluded. Tight. If this Mr. Hayashi wanted more specifics, a list was prepared, and she had Eric's agreement to negotiate pricing details.

"It'll be a delicate transaction," Eric had said. "You'll arrive in Tokyo on Monday. By Tuesday night you'll have met Hayashi in his office and worked things out. Because you've always wanted to visit Japan, on Wednesday you'll ride the Bullet Train to Kyoto. You're booked for two nights into a traditional Japanese inn. Then you'll fly back to San Francisco."

Everything will be fine, she assured herself as she stared through the window at the ocean below—flat, gray, infinite. I'll present my contract between Oriental Tours and the Hayashi Corporation, listen to proposed changes, weigh them, make suggestions in a firm but nonthreatening manner, include only what won't adversely affect my client. Negotiate as usual and hope it works in Japan.

Early in her legal career, Chelsea Jarvis figured the best way to deal with difficult people and tough situations was to look as if she understood them completely and knew exactly what to do. During business hours, she appeared calm, stress-free, underneath on complete guard, knowing if caught in a confused state she would lose control and the attorney who lost control would lose the case. Especially—and she had seen this happen—if the attorney was a woman.

Replacing the contract, she snapped the briefcasecase shut. The sound caught the attention of the same man as before. With a defiant move, she shoved the briefcase under the seat in front of her.

The attendant dropped a hot perfumed towel on her tray. Methodically, Chelsea cleansed her hands. As soon as she set the towel down, it was whisked away. A meal appeared, chicken teriyaki and rice. She was hungrier than she realized. Another hot towel followed. The same ritual. The long flight ahead was like facing eternity.

Yanking up her briefcase again, she pulled out her laptop and reviewed notes for the Thompson case she would try next month. An hour passed. Enough of that, she decided, jamming the laptop back and once more stowing the briefcase under the seat, feeling the eyes of the man across the aisle. She frowned. Doesn't he have anything better to do than stare at my every move? For a few moments, she stretched her legs. Okay, what'll I do now?

She didn't care to watch a movie on her private screen. The only available choices were explosive thrillers and sappy romances; she preferred foreign films. She slipped off her shoes, hoping that would relax her body.

A second meal appeared. She ate the salad, ignored the steak and drank the wine. Three quarters of the way into the long flight she fell asleep. Waking with a jerk, she glanced at her watch, surprised she had slept for nearly three hours.

At last the plane edged downward. She tucked the reading glasses into her shirt pocket, squeezed into her high heels, snatched up her suit jacket from the empty seat beside her and punched her arms into the sleeves. Shouldering her black purse and with chin held high, she charged up the aisle to repair her makeup.

As she stared into the bathroom mirror to apply fresh lipstick, she wondered why she couldn't control her bangs. Damned things sprouted like weeds. Odd, since the rest of her hair grew in an orderly fashion. With a shrug, she brushed a piece of lint off her right sleeve, buttoned her jacket and adjusted her hat. She made certain the Japanese dictionary was in her left pocket.

I'm ready, she informed her reflection. Success with this agreement could coax out future business. Probably Eric wanted to test her ability to operate in foreign territory. Whatever his motive, this was a respite from kowtowing to angry judges and slimy insurance adjusters.

When she heard the announcement for landing, her uneasiness returned. Why had Eric insisted she go to Tokyo alone? Why right away? Why ask her to negotiate this contract when always before he had handled them? Was he sending her to Japan for another reason?

CHAPTER 2

As she came out of Customs, a bespectacled Japanese man, red flower in his buttonhole, stepped forward, bowed and handed her a note: *Welcome to Japan, Ms. Jarvis. Give this man your baggage-claim ticket. Then proceed through the terminal's main door and look for Tamiyasu-san, my chauffeur. He, too, will wear a red flower. He will bring you to my office first and then to your hotel.* The note was signed with a red seal.

She allowed herself to be swept along with the crowd that funneled toward the exit doors, realizing, since she was taller than most, she could maintain control when necessary. Once outside the terminal, she made a determined stand and the crowd flowed past her.

God, it was hot. Her skin felt clammy, her eyes burned. Wasn't April supposed to be cool? Why did Hayashi want her to come to the office first? A rest at the hotel would be preferable. She listened to the jumbled voices of the crowd, drowned out at sixty-second intervals by the roar of planes. At first she was amused, thinking it sounded like an operatic recitative, then annoyed, then resigned, in quick order. Beyond the mob she glimpsed a white limousine drawn up to the curb. Next to it, stiff as a mannequin, stood a Japanese man, head and shoulders above the crowd. He wore a dark suit with a red flower in the buttonhole. He held a card with large, bold print: *Ms. Jarvis*. She edged forward, using her briefcase as a buttress—a courthouse tactic.

"I'm Chelsea Jarvis," she announced when she arrived a few feet away from the man. He stood on a plastic stool which brought him up to her height. His face seemed carved from a chunk of alder. A disquieting idea struck her: he might not be human. She said, "Tamiyasu-san?"

"*Hai! Hai!*" He spoke explosively with jerking bows.

Remembering *hai* meant *yes,* and considering the possibility he spoke no English, she set her briefcase on the pavement and fished for the dictionary, thumbing through the thin pages to find the word for *suitcase*. She had to let him know about the other Japanese man wearing the red flower, the guy who was picking up her bag.

She squinted at the fine print, realizing she should have left her glasses on. Nuts! *Suitcase* wasn't in there. She flipped back through the pages and searched for the word *baggage*. "*Nimotsu?*" she said finally, looking up.

The stool was empty. Where was he? There, opening the back door to the limousine.

"*Nimotsu, nimotsu!*" she called to him. The noise of the crowd and the planes was deafening. Of course he couldn't hear her. He was too far away. She could barely hear herself. Stuffing the dictionary back into her pocket, she grasped her briefcase and rushed over to him. "*Nimotsu, kudasai,*" she cried, pointing to herself and then at the terminal. She searched the crowd in hopes the man with her suitcase magically would appear. "*Otoko,*" she over-enunciated the word for *man*. Screwing up her face, she tried to remember how to say, *I wonder where he is?*

His face was a mask, his eyes were glass. He shook his head, bowed and gestured for her to enter the back seat.

Surely the guy must understand she couldn't leave the terminal without her suitcase. The words for the question she wanted to ask flashed across her mind. "*Doko e itta desho ka?*" she shouted.

Tamiyasu's eyebrows shot up. He drew a load of breath in between his teeth, a reversed hiss.

"*Nimotsu! Doko desu ka,*" she yelled down into his face.

With a guttural grunt, he backed off as if fearful she might attack him. Then seeming to understand, he nodded and leaned forward. "*Ato de hoteru ni todoke masu.*"

"*Ato?*" She thumbed the pages, but when he broke into a torrent of Japanese, she gave up on the dictionary and closed her eyes, determined to make sense of it. Something about her hotel. Something about later. Something about…it seeped through. Her suitcase was going to be delivered to her hotel room.

Her shoulders slumped. Here she was, battered by noise in a foreign throng, scarcely able to think. She couldn't remember the word for *bathroom* and soon that would be a problem. With a weak smile, she opened her eyes and said, "*Gomen nasai,*" but doubted if her apology could be heard for the airport noise had risen to Wagnerian levels. Not knowing what else to do, she bowed.

A smile brushed across his face. He returned her bow and once more gestured for her to enter the limousine. She retrieved her briefcase and attempted to look dignified as she climbed into the black leather interior.

The moment the door closed, all airport sounds disappeared. Although glad of the glass partition between front and back seats, eliminating further need to talk with the chauffeur, she didn't like being isolated.

I need air, she thought, swallowing hard. Can't breathe in here. Must open windows. How? No buttons. No handles. No knobs, levers—nothing on the doors.

Trapped. Imprisoned.

She straightened her hat and tried to calm down. Reaching into her purse, she dug for a wipe-and-dry packet and tore it open as if it were a life-saving necessity.

Cool air rushed from vents near the floor. Music floated through speakers behind her. Relieved, she patted her forehead and neck with the wet tissue.

It's okay, she told herself, leaning back. Although it did seem weird to be listening to *Clair de Lune* in Japan while beyond the smoky glass partition a little man from an alien culture checked the limousine's instruments as if piloting a space ship.

A loud snap.

She flinched.

The sound issued from a speaker below the glass partition. Tamiyasu's voice crackled out, *"Yoroshii desho ka?"*

She leaned toward the speaker, found a button beneath it and pressed. *"Daijobu,"* she answered to assure him she was fine.

The limousine drive, starting as an artful weave through heavy traffic, soon slowed to a bumper to bumper crawl among cars, mostly white, black or navy blue, an occasional bright color. Along the highway rose apartment complexes, factories, resort areas, high rises, road signs. The limousine crept toward a toll gate. They inched forward in the long line.

Eric should have come with her, she thought as she stared at the traffic through the limousine window. He wasn't Japanese, but he was fluent in the language and understood the culture, having lived in Japan most of his life. His father was attached to the American Embassy in Tokyo until he died. Yes, Eric should be here.

"At the moment I'm too tied up," he had told her. Then, as if remembering their discussions a few weeks earlier, he added, "Another time, honey, yes, yes, we'll go there together for sure."

She wasn't sure it would ever happen.

Their first meeting had occurred a year ago in the court house rotunda. Eric had recently flown back from Tokyo to San Francisco, his birthplace, and Chelsea stood by an automatic coffee machine, sipping a cup.

"You a lawyer?" he asked.

She nodded curtly. "McCloskey, Warner and Jarvis." She handed him her card. "I'm Jarvis." She started to add that the firm was small but decided against it.

With an engaging grin, he said, "If you're as good as you look, I might hire you."

He returned with her to the law offices. Over several days, she drew up the legal documents to establish his travel agency as a corporation. Eric was charming, funny, upbeat, a few inches shorter than she, but so what. They shared meals and park walks; three weeks after meeting, they slept together.

His business grew fast. She was proud to have started his corporation, happy to have a self-sufficient boyfriend. Even so, she maintained a separate residence. Although she seldom made legal mistakes, often she had been careless in her private life. The last episode involved a lover whose ego needed constant fortification. This time she was determined to keep a surface relationship until she understood the man. But a year later she still didn't have a complete handle on him, never knew what he might do next. In the courtroom she was adept at figuring people out. Not Eric.

It was dusk now. The limousine moved faster, a traffic jam in the opposite direction. The roadside was deluged with neon signs for pachinko parlors and karaoke bars and western intrusions such as Kentucky Fried Chicken and McDonalds. Interspersed were glimpses of the small unpainted wooden buildings she associated with Japan. Every block had a myriad of brightly lit vending machines and brilliant billboards—vivid pictures, bold graphics, accompanied by vertical lines of black characters in kanji and hiragana, sometimes with English translations—advertisements for food, cosmetics, hotels, machines—Nissan, Mitsubishi, Sony. The signs seemed to stretch out until she saw them as elongated ribbons of light, rippling, curving. Chopin wafted through the car. She closed her eyes and listened, comforted by the link to her world.

Ten minutes later she opened her eyes, surprised that the signs were gone. She pressed her face against the glass pane and peered up at window-lit skyscrapers, jutting into a charcoal-colored night sky that hung down like a gauze curtain. Along both sides of the street were pruned trees, evenly spaced, all the same height, their tops like green pompons. Not like any species she knew. She swallowed hard and thought, I better be careful. It's an unknown world out there.

CHAPTER 3

The limousine stopped in front of a tall office building. Tamiyasu scurried to open the passenger door, then bowed.

The sounds of snarling traffic hit Chelsea like a shock wave. Not as loud as the airport but a sharp contrast to the silent interior. She took a deep breath and blew it out before emerging into the smoggy Tokyo evening. Solemn men in business suits, their briefcases carried as if full of diamonds, filed in and out of the gray marble building. It was eight o'clock.

"Arigato gozaimasu, Tamiyasu-san" she said cheerfully, bowing to the bowing man. She grasped her briefcase and wondered if she should give him a tip. Before she could decide, he scooted away and climbed behind the steering wheel.

For a few moments she watched the limousine join the stream of traffic, then faced the building. On the steps stood another Japanese gentleman with a red flower in his lapel. He bowed lower than Tamiyasu. She bowed back, knowing points were made with this bowing business.

Her mind back on alert, chin high, she marched up the steps, following her latest contact into the marble building, matching his cadence, aware that most men she passed were shorter than she, several pausing, unable to hide their astonishment.

How do they see me? As an overgrown Dorothy, approaching the Wizard of Oz? A female Gulliver among Lilliputians? Repressing a smile, she concluded it was more likely they saw her as a monster from a Nintendo game.

An attractive secretary buzzed her into Hayashi's office. He sat behind a huge teak desk. Except in photos of Sumo wrestlers, Chelsea had never seen such a heavy person. His head looked glued onto his bulging body. The moment the door closed in back of her, he rose to his feet, steadying himself with the desk, and came forward to greet her. He wore formal attire—black cutaway coat, striped pants and white gloves.

"Welcome to Japan, Ms. Jarvis." He spoke slowly, each word enunciated as if it were a gift. His bow was slight, a dip of the head, eyes closed. "I hope your journey was not too exhausting."

"The long flight allowed me to prepare for a coming-up trial." She indicated her briefcase.

"How wise to utilize your time."

Although his smile was wide, his eyes looked cold and shrewd. Obeying his gesture, she sat down on the pale green couch that matched the thick carpet.

It was an impressive office. Shoji screens covered the wall of windows and continued across the sides of the room. On a corner of Hayashi's desk, softly spot-lit from the ceiling, was a square vase of red peonies, the same kind of flowers in the buttonholes of her three contacts. A low teak table divided the couch from a large chair upholstered in green and gold brocade.

Adjusting the back of his coat, he lowered himself onto the chair. His smile remained in place while his eyes appraised her as if trying to understand the relationship between what she wore—the severely tailored teal blue suit and black hat—and her face and figure—extremely feminine. It was an incongruity she used advantageously in her profession.

A rap on the door.

"Dozo," Hayashi called.

A girl, twenty or so, wearing a white blouse and navy skirt, entered carrying a tray. Kneeling at one end of the low table, she set the tray down and carefully placed one of the cups before

Hayashi and the other before Chelsea. In a graceful manner, the girl poured the green tea. Leaving the pot on the tray, she rose as easily as a ballerina and bowed.

"Tea is a tradition in our country," Hayashi announced as he watched the girl leave the room. "We have adopted modern ways, but never shall we give up the tea."

"Nor the bowing," Chelsea added.

Hayashi removed his gloves. "One must show respect."

"Indeed. One must."

He gave a little grunt of approval and picked up his cup with both hands.

Silently they sipped tea and nibbled rice cakes.

He poured more tea for them both. On they sipped and nibbled, while he smilingly observed her hat, her face, and her briefcase and she studied the room, eyeing him surreptitiously, wondering how much longer this show of respect and tradition would continue. She was grateful that the receptionist had led her to a bathroom before this meeting.

The rice cake tasted overly sweet, but the green tea was refreshing and the thin porcelain cups and the teapot were painted with a charming scene of cormorants on a river overhung with branches of red flowers. The couch was comfortable, the environment serene. Let him introduce their business, she decided. She could wait as long as necessary.

At last he set his cup down, slowly wiped his hands on one of the two, damp, perfumed napkins on the tea tray, and then gestured at her briefcase as if casting magic powder. "Have you completed the agreement?"

"Of course." She wiped her hands on the other damp cloth and brought out the file. Opening the folder, she removed the agreement and handed it to him with a flourish.

He pursed his lip and lifted his eyebrows as if he found her actions amusing.

"Mr. Hunter has already signed," she said, slightly annoyed at his condescending manner. "As you know, this is an agreement between Oriental Tours, an American corporation, and Hayashi Associates, a Japanese corporation. You, as corporate president, agree that Oriental Tours has the exclusive right to handle all plans and contingencies for your people traveling to, from and within the United States. My client, as President of Oriental Tours, agrees to give you and your people full cooperation, and he will personally attend to details to make each trip comfortable and successful; you'll find those details itemized on page three. Of course, he will need the retainer fee as specified."

She waited for a reaction, noting his gloves were on again.

He read the top sheet. After a few minutes he thumbed through the next two pages, pausing at the last page, where he appeared to scrutinize the signature. His nod was slow. "I see no problem with this." He looked up at her and smiled.

She said, "The fees—are the amounts agreeable?"

"Certainly."

"The retainer?"

"I will wire the money tomorrow."

"Do you have any questions, Mr. Hayashi? Would you like more details?"

"No."

This was not what she had expected. Surely he would want time limits set, more itemization, the fees negotiated.

"Perhaps," she said, "you would like to think about this. You may wish to keep the agreement until tomorrow so you can discuss the stipulations with your attorney or consult with your board of directors."

He shook his head. "That is not necessary. I can see you have prepared a simple, straight-forward agreement, fair and honest."

With some difficulty he stood and moved to his desk. He sank heavily into the chair and took the pen from its brass holder.

"Do you have a notary," she asked quickly, "or someone who will act as a witness?"

"Your client knows my signature and respects it."

"But—"

"There are other ways of authenticating a signature, Ms. Jarvis. You are in Japan." He signed the last page.

She frowned, bothered by the ease of the transaction. Eric certainly hadn't needed her for this. "Hammer out an agreement," he had said. No hammer needed. And a signature without a notary or a witness? Not the usual kind of business deal. What was going on here?

From an inner pocket, Hayashi removed a key attached to a thin gold chain that rolled out like a tape measure. His head disappeared below the desk. She heard a lock turn and a drawer open. A large, thick, manila envelope appeared on top of the desk. The drawer closed and the lock turned. His smiling head returned to view and the key slipped back into his pocket.

"I have a request," he said as he opened the lid of a shallow brass box to his right. He lifted out a small, red, oblong block.

"Yes?" she said, wondering what the block was. It looked like a chunk of wax.

A tiny flame shot up from a metal lighter in his left hand. He held the fire against the end of the block and crimson drops fell like blood onto the last page of the agreement and then onto the manila envelope. Extinguishing the flame, he set the lighter aside and returned the red block to its place, picking up another oblong item next to it, this one wood or metal. With abrupt movements, he pressed the object on the two sets of congealed drops.

His stamp, she realized.

Hayashi returned the stamp to the box and snapped the lid shut.

She felt the need to speak. "You said you had a request."

"Yes, a small favor." He pushed himself up and brought the agreement and the manila envelope over. He set the agreement on the low teak table and held the manila envelope out to her. "Please deliver this to Mr. Hunter. I was going to mail it to him, but as long as you are here...."

"Sure, all right," she said, taking the envelope. "Is that all?"

He nodded. "Inside is an important document, Ms. Jarvis, so be most careful with it."

"I'm always careful. Is Eric...I mean Mr. Hunter...is he expecting this?"

Hayashi nodded and returned to his desk where he pushed a button on a speaker. "*Tamiyasu-san, oyobinasai.*"

"*Hai!*" replied a female voice.

Chelsea picked up the manila envelope, legal-size, not heavy but thick, indicating numerous pages inside. As she stored it in her briefcase, she noted the design on the wax that sealed the envelope. Hayashi certainly had a thing for red peonies. She checked Hayashi's signature on the agreement, then filed it away.

Surely this wasn't why Eric had wanted her to come here. It had been too simple a transaction. Again she glanced at the wax seal on the manila envelope before snapping her briefcase shut.

She stood up.

Hayashi came forward. With feet together and hands behind his back, he bowed stiffly. "I appreciate your visit, Ms. Jarvis. Your agreement is excellent"—his smile widened—"and your hat most intriguing."

"*Do mo arigato,*" she said. "*Shitsurei shimasu.*"

Their eyes met, a quick exchange of curiosity.

"*Sayonara,*" he said.

"*Sayonara,*" she replied, her bow matching his, her smile, she hoped, just as inscrutable.

CHAPTER 4

Soft music wafted and the air conditioner hummed as Mr. Tamiyasu drove Chelsea along crowded streets. When they arrived at the small, two-story Senryu Hotel, a tiny, bent-over lady bustled out to their car, bowing many times and crying "*Irasshaimase*" as if welcoming a highly honored guest.

In the foyer behind a counter, a gray-haired gentleman in a dark blue suit spoke to her, his English careful. "Ms. Jarvis, your check-in forms are complete." With the authoritative look of a priest, he handed a key to her and gestured toward the elevator. "Tea awaits in your room and your bath is drawn. Rest well, please." He clasped his hands and concluded with the inevitable bow.

"Who checked me in?" she asked, surprised the hotel didn't require her signature.

He tilted his head. "I only know it has been done."

"Don't you need my passport number?"

"I believe we have it." He pulled a card from a file. "Yes. Everything is here." With both hands he held the card for her to see. "Is this correct?"

She rummaged through her purse, found her passport and compared the numbers. Everything matched. Also listed on the card was the office issuing her passport, her home address and phone numbers, the date and place of her birth, her law firm, its location, e-mail, phone and fax numbers.

"Correct," she said, her brows drawn.

The little bent-over lady reached for the briefcase with the apparent intent of carrying it. Chelsea smiled, shook her head and strode toward the elevator. All the silent way to the second floor, she had the disquieting sense of swimming in an undertow. Some people in Tokyo knew a lot about her, while she knew nothing about them.

Her concerns faded as she entered her room. A peaceful haven in pale blue and cream. Brahms issued from the ceiling although she saw no sign of speakers. The radio itself was subtly integrated into the bamboo headboard. Perhaps music from Western-style classicals was played frequently in Japan. Or was it used only for foreigners as a comforting touch? Studying the shoji screens across the windows and the closet, she decided their simplicity and the effect of muted light added restfulness to a room.

On a small table, a gold lacquered tray held a blue porcelain teapot, matching cup, two rice cookies, and a napkin folded in the shape of a butterfly. In the painting above the bed, a kimonoed lady stood on an arched bridge, her body gracefully bent to one side, face hidden by a parasol.

The only intrusion into the room's perfection was her black suitcase, the roll-on delivered from the airport as promised—an ugly monolith. Quickly she transferred it into the closet, set her briefcase and purse down beside it and slid the shoji shut. There, a perfect scene.

She lifted the lid to the teapot and peered inside. Full. Hot. In the bathroom the tub was filled, steam rising toward a ceiling fan. She tested the water. Exceedingly hot. Whoever drew the bath knew the precise time to do it. Also, the teapot could not have been filled more than a few minutes before her entrance. Uncanny timing. Invisible people were slipping in and out of her life at proper moments, performing tasks to sooth her body and spirit, people who knew what she needed.

When she returned to the bedroom, she noticed an envelope on the dresser, her name and room number on it in precise handwriting—Eric's. She was certain of it. Inside were details about her sojourn in Japan: explicit transportation arrangements; the itinerary of her tour in Tokyo the day after her arrival; the name of the Kyoto inn, the Momiji-ya where she would stay for two nights; the temples she would visit in Nara; a concluding section on how she would return to the airport with her Kyoto guide, a man by the name of Kagawa.

The music was Brahms' *Lullaby*. Abruptly, she crossed to the headboard and switched the radio off.

Had Eric mailed this letter to the hotel? No, to mail it would have run the risk of it not arriving in time. He could have faxed or e-mailed the information, but this was his ink signature. Why hadn't he given her the letter in San Francisco?

Two days ago, Eric had made a surprised appearance in her office—that hadn't happened since he'd signed his corporation documents.

The afternoon had been a bad one for Chelsea. Her client, Joe Baynor, an accused drug dealer, had sauntered into court for his arraignment ten minutes late. Chelsea had talked Judge Thorpe into waiting for him, something she hated to do, knowing how busy his docket was. Joe's nonchalant manner seemed to anger the judge, and when Joe started to explain about traffic jams and too many people in this world, Chelsea had to silence him with an authoritative command to enter his plea and be quiet. Later, outside the courtroom, she said, "Joe, if you don't shape up, I won't handle your case." He looked chagrinned and promised. She didn't believe him.

At 3:15, as she sat back at her desk dictating answers to a seemingly interminable set of Interrogatories, a fat lady with purple-tinted hair invaded the office, shouting obscenities, insisting her personal injury case wasn't being pursued to the full extent of the law. Chelsea rose to her full height. "You're not one of my clients," she snapped. "Please leave." The woman left, still ranting, and burst into McCloskey's office.

Then an insurance adjuster arrived, purportedly to discuss settlement, instead inquiring about Chelsea's sex life. At 4:30 she remembered she must get to the Court House before 5:00 to file a Summons and Complaint or the Statue of Limitations would run out. By 5:15, back in the office, she had the notion her bones were disintegrating and her mind might explode.

Trying to recover, she swiveled in her desk chair toward the window and stared sullenly at a band of fog that surrounded the dome of the Court House like a funeral wreath. She heard her office door open. Lips pressed, prepared for another confrontation, she swung her chair around. There stood Eric.

"Why are you in my office?" she inquired. "And why back so soon from Japan?"

He sat down in the client's chair. "I've come to proposition you."

"I accept."

He chuckled. "It's not what you think. I'm offering you a vacation in Japan."

"Want me to drum up business for your travel agency?"

"No, it's a legal matter. I need you to fly to Tokyo. Meet with the head of a large corporation. Hammer out an agreement for Oriental Tours."

"Why didn't you do it while you were there?" she asked.

"Didn't think I should. Could be a difficult transaction and I don't know about legal stuff."

She leaned back in her chair. "I've heard Japanese executives don't like to do business with woman lawyers."

"This executive is different. After the meeting, I'll arrange for you to go to Kyoto for a few days. Book you into a tradtionally-styled inn, a *ryokan*, to experience Japanese culture. Spring is a great time to visit temples and gardens. You've always wanted to go to Japan. Here's your chance.

"Sounds terrific."

"I want you to go this Wednesday."

"What? Today's Monday. I'd have to reschedule clients, change depositions. I've got a trial in two weeks."

"Take your case notes with you."

"I don't even know if my passport's up-to-date."

"I'll help with everything. The sooner you go, the better for me." He cleared his throat. "It'll do you good—a break from the grind."

"If I go, will you come with me?"

"No, I can't. Not now." Again he cleared his throat. "Look, I'll drop over tonight with a bottle of wine—a good Bordeaux."

Her eyes narrowed. She had detected an uncharacteristic nervousness in his voice. For a moment she toyed with the glass paper weight on her desk. "What time tonight?"

"Eight."

"Okay. But no promises until I hear the details."

Eric had arrived at her condo exactly at eight. With the assistance of the Bordeaux and a romantic evening, he had convinced her to fly to Japan.

That night she had asked him about her itinerary. "Don't worry, he replied. "You'll be well cared for—no problems with food, lodging or transportation. Then, at the airport, "I'll make sure that a complete schedule awaits you in Tokyo. Have a great time," followed by a light kiss and a disarming grin as he waved her off.

Well, here was the schedule. Eric must have drawn it up and dropped it off at the hotel before he left Japan. He knew he could talk her into going, knew it before asking her. Preplanned her transportation, hotel reservations, guides—everything.

In what other ways had he manipulated her? Was Eric Hunter, the charming joker, suave lover, calm eye, also the clever operator of her life? No indication before this. Who decided where to go? What to eat? Who to visit? When to have sex? Joint decisions. If manipulation was necessary, she was the one who used it. If otherwise, surely she would've been aware of it.

The thought of being used was abhorrent to her, especially when she didn't understand a reason for it. And right now it was even more offensive because she was in foreign territory.

I'm in control of this situation, she told herself, placing her hat on the dresser.

No, you're not, she replied and sat down on the edge of the bed.

Then I better be exceedingly careful until I am.

She didn't know the ground rules here and suspected she wouldn't like them if she did. The agreement with Hayashi could be a front, a decoy, a concocted purpose to hide the real one. So far, the only other detected reason was to bring a manila envelope back to Eric. "A small favor," Hayashi had said. "I was going to mail it to him, but as long as you are here...."

Perhaps Hayashi hadn't planned to mail it. The envelope might contain something that couldn't be mailed.

Dope?

She slid back the closet shoji, opened her briefcase as if it were made of glass, and carefully drew out the manila envelope. Flat. Legal size. About an inch and a half thick, similar to the weight of a three-hour deposition. She pressed all parts of the envelope and attempted to bend it but the package was too thick. No indication of staples, paper clips or binding. Except for the outer seal, no protrusions. She held the envelope up to her ear and shook it. Methodically, she felt, bent, rattled and smelled the envelope just to be certain.

If only she could look inside. But to break the seal would be a trespass, an intrusion into private business. All her legal training contended such an act could not be condoned. She wasn't a shady lawyer, for God's sake. Besides, Eric would realize she had opened it.

She replaced the envelope in her briefcase and snapped the lock shut. Had Eric sent her to Japan just to bring back this envelope? If so, why? What made it so valuable? Or was it? Maybe it was only travel information and she was here for another purpose.

She would call Eric now. Insist he tell her why she was here. She started to get her cell phone from her purse.

No. She closed the closet shoji.

I'm too tired. I'll wait. No need to get immediate answers. I'll sip tea, luxuriate in a bath and then go down to the hotel restaurant and order sushi. Tonight, a long sleep—the most important ingredient for anyone in a precarious position. Tomorrow morning at ten Mr. Tamiyasu will arrive, bringing with him an English-speaking guide to escort me around Tokyo. Then two days in Kyoto, staying in a ryokan. She liked the sound of its name—Momiji-ya. Exotic. Mysterious.

"Relax!" she whispered ferociously at herself in the mirror. "It's your vacation. Take advantage of it."

She knew, though, that her mind would continue to operate, attempting to solve what she didn't understand, mental currents probing through hidden files—part of the training.

"What would my life have been like as a topless dancer?" she asked her reflection. "Then I could simply concentrate on movement."

During the summers when she was eighteen and nineteen, she had worked as a topless dancer in a sleazy joint on Broadway, gaining enough money to go back to college. Easy work. No mental demands. She had been good at it.

No longer did she use the movements of her body to raise fires in men. Instead she relied on her mind. She considered herself an expert at handling icebergs—obstacles with more below the surface than most people realized. She smiled wryly at herself in the mirror, took a gulp of tea and burned her tongue.

CHAPTER 5

Tsuyoshi Moore knelt on a pillow on the floor of his Grandmother's house. "My mother might return to Kyoto," he said to her. "For a visit, I mean. If she does, I am sure she would like to see you again."

He was aware he had used his university lecture voice. Wrong here, he realized. Wrong in this small room of tatami mats and rice paper screens, especially wrong in front of this fragile, old Japanese woman who knelt on the other side of the low table. Even his choice of words had been a mistake, a set of cold variables. And his gift, the wrapped box of chocolates, a crass object beside her lovely tea set. He plodded on, "But my mother is... well...she's afraid to come."

"No reason to fear," the old woman said. She set her half-filled cup of tea down as if it needed extra care.

He cleared his throat. The green pillow on which he knelt felt like a lily pad—too small and delicate. He was sinking. He adjusted his knees, breathed deeply and exhaled slowly.

Even more disturbing to him was the awkwardness of his body. How could he maintain this kneeling position? His suit felt like armor, his tie, a noose. He shouldn't have gulped his tea nor refused the second cup, and he should've tried to speak in Japanese because it seemed her knowledge of English was slight. He knew he wasn't handling this meeting well, and he desperately wished he could disappear and start over again.

Determined to remain calm, he examined the flower arrangement in the alcove: a branch of corkscrew willow, two peonies, one open, one closed. On the wall behind hung a long scroll, a poem or famous saying he supposed. He glanced back at Grandmother, modest, yet quietly elegant, kneeling on the other side of the low table. "My mother thinks—"

Grandmother lowered her eyes.

He charged on. "She thinks you don't want to see her."

The old woman turned her head slightly to one side as if to digest his words. "I not understand."

"I mean, when she didn't marry a Japanese man, married my father instead and ran off to America, you were angry."

She shook her head and folded her hands into the sleeves of her kimono. "I not angry. Husband angry. I sad."

"But you never answered her letters."

A sigh escaped like a bewildered moth. She barely whispered, "Husband say no write." Another small sigh. "Husband in Tokyo now. Home very little. Tell Yumiko, come, please."

"Yes, of course. I'll give Mother your message."

She nodded but didn't look up.

Although Tsuyoshi had read book after book about the old culture and could speak the language, not fluently but well enough to be understood, he hadn't expected to encounter traditional Japan in anybody's home, let alone be involved with it. He had heard the Japan was fast becoming westernized, which was why he had booked himself into a ryokan, believing an inn would be the only place he could touch his fast-disappearing heritage. The inn was not as traditional as Grandmother's house.

Her head remained bowed, a discreet glance now and then from the tops of her eyes. She must consider him an oaf. Even if he could redo this meeting, smooth it out, he knew he would be compelled to stare at her.

He sipped his tea.

There she knelt, a small, delicate figure, spine curved like a willow branch, face serene. With her head bowed most of the time, it was her hair he mainly saw, snow white, rising into a neatly sculptured bun, a black lacquer pin protruding from one side. In those moments she fully revealed her face, he found it hard to believe. Her skin was tissue-paper white and unusually smooth for a woman in her eighties. She wore a dark blue kimono, white edging along the v-neck, a gray obi wrapped tightly around her waist. She was different from anyone he had known.

He had expected an older version of his mother, who had lost her Japanese heritage or tried to hide it—her clothes, makeup, haircut and all more American.

"Your father named you Tsuyoshi," his mother had once informed him, brushing a crumb off the Formica drain board as if it were an obstacle in her path. "I wanted to call you Bill, Jr." She frowned. "At least you've got his six-foot height."

Had that meant she wished he hadn't inherited her Asian features—the oval eyes, the high cheekbones, the straight black hair? He never was sure how she felt.

Afternoon light filtered through the screens making the figure before him seem more like a painting.

This is my grandmother, he thought again and again, as if he had to remind himself it was true. This is a hint of what Mother might been if she had stayed in Japan. Odd to have lived 33 years and not understood this before. Strange to be here in Kyoto in a tatami-matted room, to kneel across from Grandmother for the first time.

His ideas on how people in Japan lived today had been fused from Tokyo businessmen, exchange students, newspaper articles, TV programs. What he saw and heard in his three Tokyo days confirmed his concept: people in Japan now dressed, lived, and thought much like people in America. Little difference between them and him. Not so here, and if not here, perhaps not elsewhere.

Staring into his empty cup, he told himself to remain calm. So what if he hadn't done everything perfectly? At least he had known enough to remove his shoes before coming into her house. But, awkwardly, he had grasped the edge of the shoji screen and somehow yanked it off track. While he pushed and pulled and lifted the screen in an attempt to correct the problem, sweating as if defending a dissertation, Grandmother made little sounds of "Ohhh" and "Ahhh" and raised her hands as if to say he should leave it, forget it, which of course he could not do.

On he struggled with the screen while time stretched. What probably was no more than five minutes became an hour in his mind. At last the shoji slipped back on track. He slid it open and shut several times to be certain no further catastrophe would occur. Satisfied, he forced a smile and walked inside, where Grandmother, head bowed, hands clasped at her waist, waited for him.

Noting two lily-pad pillows on either side of a low table, he had collapsed onto one. She knelt on the other pillow, her movements surprisingly fluid for a woman her age.

Although his clumsy entrance had happened forty minutes ago, his stomach still flip-flopped at the memory. He adjusted his kneeling position, wondering if this was the correct way for a Japanese man to sit. Good grief, here he was, an associate professor of English, a recognized authority on Wordsworth, feeling like a teenager meeting a prospective girlfriend's parents. His knees ached as if he was an old man. His toes felt numb; he wiggled his stocking feet on the pillow.

In a voice lower than he had yet used, one he felt was more in tune with the room and the situation, he said, "Mother will be happy, I mean to know you want her to visit."

She gave two emphatic nods.

After a long silence, he said, "I better go now." He had difficulty rising. "I'm staying at the Momiji-ya."

"M-m-m." She rose in a graceful manner.

"Shall I return tomorrow?" he ventured. "I don't want to bother you, but if you think I should, then of course I will, but perhaps I...." His words seemed to lack meaning. Not once during their conversation had he been able to convey how he felt.

"Tomorrow, four o'clock," Grandmother said. "Tea ceremony. Please, you come."

He scratched his chin. Close to panic, honesty burst out of him. "I'll make a mess of it, I don't want to embarrass you."

She waved her hands as if to brush his concerns away. "No need you worry." She pointed at her nose. "I teach you."

He swallowed hard as he realized it was important to her. "All right, I'll come."

She nodded as if to finalize the agreement. Glancing up at him she said, "You very tall man."

"My father's tall," he said.

"*Hai, hai.*" She moved across the tatami with dainty, shuffling steps and slid open the shoji screen opposite the one he had entered.

Outside was an immaculately groomed garden. Mounds of azalea bushes bloomed in shades of red. In the background large rhododendrons, their buds half open. A flowering cherry tree's reflection in the pond looked as if a pink cloud had been cast on the water. Flowers bloomed like jewels along a curved pathway.

We grow the same plants at home, he thought, but our garden doesn't look like this. More structure here, more compaction. Neater. Beyond the pond, half hidden, stood a wooden building the size of a gazebo only square and enclosed, its roof thatched.

"Tea house," she said, gesturing toward the structure. "Tomorrow four o'clock, you come. If you like, bring friend."

"I don't have a friend here. I flew to Japan by myself."

"Alone?"

"Yes."

"*Ah, so desu ka.*"

She closed the garden screen and shuffled across the room to the opposite shoji, opening it and bowing. "Goodbye."

"*Arigato,*" he said, not certain why he was thanking her.

She emitted a squeaking sound, a laugh. Her hand instantly covered her mouth. Then, she glanced up at him and whispered, "Hey, man, take it easy."

He was caught off guard. Shocked. "Grandmother, where did you learn that?"

"From your father. Years ago." Her eyes sparked mischief. "I not forget." Again she bowed.

He resisted an impulse to hug her. Instead, he bowed. "See you tomorrow, Grandmother." In an attempt to conclude the visit with decorum, he carefully stepped off the tatami platform onto the stone-floored entry. With a straight back, he aimed for the front gate.

"Shoes," she piped after him.

With an inward groan, he returned and slipped his stockinged feet into the pair of Italian loafers he had removed before entering her pristine room.

Once more, only the top of her head faced him, so he couldn't tell if she, too, was embarrassed. Perhaps she was amused. Or disgusted. Or bored with this clumsy American who unfortunately was her grandson.

"Excuse me," he muttered with a half laugh.

"Not a problem," she replied, head still bowed. Then, she looked up at him and smiled.

Their eyes met for just a moment, but long enough for him to realize she liked him, that everything between them was okay. He smiled back.

As he hurried away he said to himself, *hey man, take it easy.* Behind him, the shoji slid shut, its final tap coinciding with his release of the latch on the front gate.

CHAPTER 6

It was an hour before dinner was to be served at the low table in Tsuyoshi's room. Wearing the light green *yukata*, the kimono-type cotton robe provided by Momiji-ya, and on his feet the special kind of slippers called *tabi*, given as he entered the inn, Tsuyoshi stood by his open shoji and admired the garden through failing sunlight, the air fresh, a slight fragrance from pine needles and wet earth. A while ago, a rain shower had brought coolness to the unseasonably warm afternoon. A frog began to croak like an old man trying to clear his throat until its voice was drowned out by the deep, resonant sound of a gong, reverberating against the tile rooftops of Kyoto. He lost track of how many times it rang. Five? Or was it six?

    He laughed softly at himself, at his bumbling efforts with Grandmother, about his fears of what to do. This afternoon hadn't been so bad. Most likely she had wanted to please him as much as he wanted to please her. He shouldn't have gotten so upset about it.

    In the *ryokan* garden, a tall, slender figure walked into view, some thirty feet away from his shoji, a young woman, Caucasian, moving past a Tanyosho pine. He couldn't tell her age at this distance, but she walked with more assurance than a teenager or a person over fifty. Her hair was black, shiny, short except for the prolific bangs. When she reached the laceleaf maple, she stopped and studied the dwarfed tree, touching the wires that guided its growth. She wore the inn's green yukata and on her feet, a type of *zori*, sandals elevated with blocks of wood.

Outside his shoji rested a similar pair of zori. He had noticed them earlier when examining the shutters. What a fine idea, he thought, to relax in a yukata and tabi then slip into wooden sandals to wander about a garden. Civilized, yet natural.

She's in her early thirties, he decided, as the woman came closer then paused about ten feet away to inspect the branches of a larger maple. Even with the strange haircut, he found her attractive, intriguing. He liked the whimsical way her bangs flew in all directions and how a lustrous pearl in the lobe of her ear glowed in the final rays of sunlight. He smiled at the picture and considered it a subject for a Wordsworthian poem.

He wondered if she was alone. Probably not. Couples were the usual everywhere, entering two by two, the Noah's Ark syndrome. Sometimes he felt he was the only one left outside.

For the last four years, since his breakup with Evelyn, he had refused to look for another woman companion. Why bother to reveal himself? He would have to go through that frantic, initial business, play the hypocrite, babble silly things people felt necessary when they started a relationship—a waste of time and effort.

More and more, as months turned to years, as he increasingly isolated himself from intimacy, Tsuyoshi believed he only cared to know women the way he knew men, through academics. Now at the age of thirty-eight, ensconced in the scholar's world, he felt safe. It was a home that held meaning, a stable retreat, a place uncluttered by the kind of emotions that clouded the mind.

The woman turned and saw him.

He found it necessary to swallow yet impossible to do.

"Hi," she called. "Do you speak English?"

"Of course," he croaked, "I'm an American."

"Sorry. I didn't mean to insult you."

"You didn't."

"One shouldn't assume. However, this is Japan, and you look Japanese." She surveyed the maple. "I should've guessed, though. You're taller than most, and you didn't bow."

"I'm half Japanese," he almost shouted, then, softer, "My mother was born here."

"Good for her," she tossed back, "and lucky for you."

He laughed, surprising himself.

She glanced over her shoulder, eyebrows arched. "What's funny?"

"Nothing, really." He cleared his throat. "Did you come to Japan on a tour?"

"No! I despise tours."

"My turn to apologize."

She touched a branch. "People trade insults when they know nothing about each other. It's the style these days."

"Not my style," he said.

She turned to face him and seemed to be assessing the value of continuing the conversation.

He stood in the doorway and thought he should slide the shoji shut and disappear into the shadows of his room.

"My name's Chelsea Jarvis," she said at last. "I'm in Japan on business." She raked her fingers through her bangs and gave him a wily look. "Would you care for a transitory friendship." She pressed her lips together. "You see, I'm a bit lonely at the moment."

"Me, too," he said quickly, "lonely, that is."

Had he really said that? Somehow he got the *zori* correctly onto his feet. Attempting to be casual, he sauntered forward, right hand outstretched. "I'm Tsuyoshi Moore, Yoshi for short." When he shook her hand, he noted her grip was firm and her height was the same as his. "I teach English Literature at the University of Washington."

"English Lit? Isn't that unusual for someone part Japanese?"

"I suppose so. Is it wrong to be unusual?"

"Certainly not." She looked amused. "I've heard it rains all the time in Seattle."

"Not as much as most people think. We have a lot of mist and overcast."

Again she inspected the branch. "Your first time in Japan?"

He nodded. "I'm here on Spring Break. Arrived in Kyoto yesterday."

"My first time, too. I spent the last few days in Tokyo. What an expensive, congested city! When I walked around the Ginza

I felt as if I'd fallen into a deep pit with half of Japan pressing in on me."

"A pit, all right." He glanced around the empty garden, hoping someone would join them.

"This morning," she continued, "I took the Bullet Train." Her hand whipped through the air to indicate its speed. "Ft-t-t!"

His eyebrows shot up.

She grinned. "I like to surprise people. I'm a lawyer."

"Oh." He had no idea what to say next. Words were coming harder. He would rather just look at her, enjoy her from a distance or hide and listen to her talk. Sweat gathered under his arms. In an effort to air himself, he raised his elbows. Realizing the move looked like a chicken ready to flap its wings, he turned it into an arm stretch to the side, out and in, twice.

"Any particular reason why you came to Japan?" she asked. "Are you heritage hunting? Out to see the scenery? A temple freak? Mind my asking questions?"

"Not at all. I'm visiting relatives. People I've never met before."

In a sedate manner he swung his arms back and forth as if exercising shoulder stiffness. Noting her eyes pinned on his motions, he lowered his arms, thinking to hell with the sweat.

"Curiosity," he continued, "I suppose that's the reason why I came. Wanted to meet my mother's people. See we had anything in common. Today I met my honorable grandmother for the first time.

"How was that?"

"I botched it. Yanked her shoji off its track and rushed from her house without my shoes."

As if to hide a smile, she looked down and smoothed a wrinkle from her yukata. "You must've made an impression."

He groaned.

"It's always worse in your mind," she said quickly.

"I hope so. She's a lovely lady. Don't want her to regret having me for a grandson." He found himself more relaxed, doing a few arm rolls. The sweat was disappearing. He glanced at her, noticing her eyes were green. Vivid. They lit up her face, an oval with a pointed chin. The jumble of black bangs topped her head like an explosion. If she were two feet shorter she might be a pixie.

"Are you into physical fitness?" she inquired.

"What?"

"You know, jogging, weight-lifting."

His arms froze in mid air. "Why do you ask?"

"Those arm movements of yours. I thought maybe you—"

"To tell you the truth, I was sweating, trying to fan away the moisture."

"Really?"

"Was that too graphic?"

A laugh erupted from her. "No. I prefer honest answers. But since the rain has made the air cooler...."

"I'm scared," he said, lowering his arms, feeling warmth in his face. "You see, I'm not in the habit of barging out for a conversation with a beautiful woman."

Their eyes met.

"Thanks," she said lightly, "for considering me a beautiful woman. And for barging out." She plucked a maple leaf from a limb and inspected it on both sides.

"Have you eaten dinner yet?" he inquired and wondered where his words came from.

"No, I'm told it's served in the room"—she glanced at her watch—"in half an hour."

The maple leaf dropped from her hand and they both watched it float to the ground.

"Perhaps we could eat together," he suggested.

Her smile was impish. "I wondered if you might come up with that notion. What's your plan? To eat in your room or mine?"

"No plan. What would you rather do?"

She gave him a squinty look.

"Dinner and conversation only," he said quietly. "I have no agenda. I'm a rather stodgy person, not at all devious."

"I believe you." There was humor in her voice. "Okay, I accept. We'll eat in your room."

As they walked toward his screen, his mind whirled with a mixture of misgivings and excitement. He doubted if this woman would care to discuss the literary giants of the Romantic Age, and he wouldn't be interested in talking about the legal profession, having long ago dismissed it as a loophole-filled, superficial world. Would they have anything in common or face each other across the low table and jabber banalities, the evening boring to them both? How had he gotten himself into this peculiar situation?

Yet he was attracted to this woman, not only her looks, but the way she spoke, her smile, her infectious laugh that seemed to bubble out, her straightforward approach. He wondered if she was naked under her yukata as he was under his. The thought made his penis rise abruptly. Good grief! This was ridiculous! *Take it easy, man,* Yoshi commanded himself.

"I'll make the arrangements," he said and rushed away to hide his growing problem. At the corner of the building he nearly fell. For God's sake, he thought, slow down. *Zori* aren't running shoes. "Go into my room," he shouted back to her. "Pour a cup of tea. Find a pillow. Relax."

CHAPTER 7

Funny guy, Chelsea thought as she walked toward Yoshi's room. Outside his shoji, she glanced about the garden with the same furtive look from her childhood, as if she were about to sneak into the drugstore to read comic books. Years later she realized no need for covert actions, for then, as now, nobody seemed to care what she did in her private life.

Her eyes widened. A man stood in the shadow of a pine tree, looking at her. It was Kagawa, the Japanese driver. He had met her at the train station this morning, drove her around to the temples and finally brought her to the inn this afternoon. How long had he been in the garden watching her? Should she wave? No. Something creepy about him.

Slipping off her zori, she stepped into Yoshi's room. When she looked back toward the tree, Kagawa was gone. Or had he melted into the shadows? A chill swept over her. Quickly she slid the screen across the doorway, closing out the garden.

It was dim inside, the only glow shining through the shoji that led to the inn's hallway, enough light for her to see Yoshi's room was a duplicate of hers. Same tatami flooring, shoji screens, low table with pit-like depression underneath for leg comfort and, on one side, a collapsible chair, more like a beach backrest, a pillow on the seat. As in her room a small TV was near the inner wall and on the table a tray with a teapot and cup.

Easing into the chair, she maneuvered her legs into the pit and then poured the tea, drank it and examined the porcelain cup as if it might reveal what would happen next.

Voices drifted down the hall. They came closer—a male conversing in Japanese with a female, the woman sounding excited, high-pitched, breathless. The screen opened and Yoshi stood there, his zori clutched in one hand. "It's all arranged," he said to Chelsea as he entered.

Behind him stood a small woman wearing a kimono, her eyes nearly squeezed shut, cheeks protruding like biscuits. She lugged a backrest and a pillow into the room.

"She wouldn't let me carry them," Yoshi whispered as if that was important to clarify.

After unfolding the backrest at the table, the woman plumped the pillow onto its seat, stood back and bowed to Yoshi.

Concern deepened on his face. He remained on the other side of the room, looking from the backrest to Chelsea to the backrest.

It hit Chelsea what his trouble was. The poor guy was nervous about sharing the pit, his knees possibly pressed against hers and sitting on the opposite side of the table, their faces only a few feet apart. She bit her lower lip to keep from smiling.

The woman hunched her shoulders and giggled into her hands. She took his zori and slipped them onto the ground outside the garden screen and then crossed to the TV, reached behind it and returned with a wrought iron lantern and a TV remote control. "*Gomen nasai,*" she apologized to Yoshi. Pursing her lips, she tapped the lantern switch. A soft light shone through the clouded glass panes.

"Ah, battery powered," Yoshi muttered as she set the lantern down on the tatami.

Holding the remote control in front of her like a weapon, the woman pressed a button. On flashed the evening news. Head bowed, smothering more giggles, she handed Yoshi the control, swept up the tea tray and fled the room, sliding the screen shut behind her.

"Yoshi," Chelsea asked, "why are you standing over there?"

"I'm not sure."

A shy man, she mused, a throwback to another age, not at all like Eric.

Apparently deciding he must come to grips with the situation, Yoshi moved forward. He edged into his chair and plunged his legs into the pit, bumping them against hers. "Sorry, I'll pull my chair this way." With bouncing hip movements, he moved to the left.

She performed a similar maneuver.

The TV news blared, blinking out pictures of a beached whale on Hachijo Island.

Sitting in their staggered positions, he faced the scroll on the wall and she faced the hallway shoji. They shot alternating glances at the TV and at each other. On the TV, the Prime Minister of Japan visited a computer company, its workers lined up in white caps and gloves.

Yoshi uttered a muffled oath and jammed his thumb onto the *off* button.

Immediate, overwhelming silence.

At the same moment, they looked at each other like a pair of startled pigeons. Both burst into laughter, Chelsea laughing so hard she collapsed sideways onto the tatami.

He said. "I seem to commit faux pas everyplace. I was afraid you'd think I was trying to..." He threw up his hands. "I still don't know what to do with my legs.

"If they're sweating, wave them in the air," she cried. The idea was so ridiculous, she fell over in another fit.

"*Gomen nasai.*" The voice came from the hall, followed by a rap on the shoji frame.

Abruptly, Chelsea sat up.

Yoshi straightened his back.

Chelsea saw the shadow of the helpful woman kneeling outside the screen.

Like children caught out of line, they quickly shifted their chairs back to the center of the table and touched knees. Slyly, Chelsea rubbed a foot against the side of his left leg, noting with glee that he blushed. To her amazement, he burrowed his right foot beneath her left foot, and kept it there. She liked it. To hell with Eric, she thought. Hell's where he deserved to go, sending her on a phony mission, keeping secrets from her, not answering the messages she left with his answering service this morning.

"*Gom kudasai?*" the woman said, her voice louder, a tone higher.

"*Hai!*" Yoshi replied. "*Ohairi nasai,*" letting her know it was all right to come on in.

Chelsea watched the screen slide back. There knelt the woman, palms flat on the tatami, bracing her body as she bowed low. In one swift, flowing movement, the woman picked up the tray in front of her and rose, gliding forward to kneel beside the table. In front of her guests she transferred two smaller trays, each containing the same prepared dishes.

Chelsea examined the contents. A set of wooden chopsticks rested on a one-inch china pedestal. Centered behind was a cup, much smaller than a teacup. Behind it, on a square dish, round, yellow slices of pickled radish, each the size of a 50 cent piece—takuan she remembered from her times eating in San Francisco's Japan Town. Artfully arranged on top of them them were brown shreds she assumed was another kind of pickle and as an accent something neon red—maybe pickled ginger. On either side, two covered bowls. Centered behind was a square dish containing what looked like a mound of compressed spinach sprinkled with sesame seeds. Farthest on the tray, a bowl of mixed vegetables and, on an oblong, six-inch plate, broiled fish decorated with a sprig of green and two raw carrot slices cut like flowers.

Ceremoniously, the woman picked up a bottle the size of a bud vase and poured hot sake into the tiny cups. She set the bottle on a wooden stand and bowed low to each guest. Rising as easily as a flag unfurling, she floated into the hall and slid the screen shut behind her.

"This is beautiful," Chelsea said, waving a hand over the table. "The way it was served, how everything looks."

"Yeah, very traditional."

"Are we supposed to look inside the covered bowls now or wait?"

"First, drink the hot sake." He picked up his cup in his left hand and sipped. "Meanwhile, use your chopsticks to eat some tsukemono—pickles." Expertly, he maneuvered the chopsticks, picking up one of the round yellow slices. It crunched as he ate it.

She followed his directions, liking the taste of the smooth, warm sake and the sharpness of the pickle.

They said nothing while they drank sake and ate tsukemono, only exchanged smiles and an occasional foot pressure.

"Let's move on to the soup," he said, resting his chopsticks on their pedestal. "I believe it's in the covered dish on your right." He removed the lid, then picked up the steaming bowl with both hands and took small swallows, watching her over the rim.

"It's miso," she said, wanting him to know she had eaten some of this food before. "Is it a bad idea to slurp the bits of tofu?" she asked after a few sips.

"Do what you like." He set the bowl down and wiggled his foot out from under. With a grin, he gently rested his feet on top of hers. "I prefer to use chopsticks."

"I'm enjoying this," she said with a straight face.

"I'm glad you're not as sophisticated as you look."

She rolled her eyes. "Well, I'm glad you speak Japanese." She spread her arms. "And glad you know about all these things. I like sharing dinner with you in this...intimate way."

His grin broadened.

She leaned forward. "Tell me, do you eat like this at home?"

He shook his head. "You'd only know my mother is Japanese by her face."

"How come you live at home with your parents?"

"I moved back last September after my sister Alice got married." He cleared his throat. "It's temporary. Mother seemed a bit forlorn. Dad suggested it, so I'm giving it a try." He fished a tofu from his soup and studied it. "To tell you the truth, at the time I also felt forlorn." He ate the cube and met her eyes. " Turns out I'm seldom at the house. I usually eat out. Don't know if I've been much of a help to her, although we've had a few good talks." He rested his chopsticks and picked up his bowl again, his voice more remote. "Mostly I eat at Japanese restaurants. I like the food, and my mother cooks only American dishes."

"I've eaten Japanese food with a friend," she said. "Sukiyaki, teriyaki, different kinds of sushi. But I've never experienced this sort of meal." She sipped the soup. "So far I like everything."

"Good."

She set her bowl down and reached over, touching his arm. "Yoshi, don't be nervous with me. I won't think badly about you or hurt you or try to corner you. I simply like your company. I'm here through tomorrow night, and if you're here during that time, let's be friends. No strings."

"I'll be here," he said, his voice husky, his eyes on her fingers.

Feeling unusually shy, she withdrew her hand. "Then, it's settled. Have you been to the ancient city of Nara?"

"No. I plan to go there in a few days."

"I have this driver, a sort of guide. He's supposed to take me there tomorrow. Will you come with me?"

He ate the last piece of tofu. "Can we return by four?"

"If it's necessary."

"It is. I have to be back by then."

She nodded. "All right, then."

"And when we come back"—he looked up—"will you go someplace with me?"

Her shoulders slumped. "Today I toured the Nijo Castle, the Golden Pavilion, the Heian Shrine and two temples. After we bombard Nara tomorrow, I doubt if I'll have the strength or desire to visit another site."

"It's nothing like that." He set his bowl down. "It's to my grandmother's house for a tea ceremony."

She straightened up. "Tea ceremony? You want me to meet your honorable grandmother in her home?" She cupped her hands in the air as if to grasp the concept. "Sure. But you'll have to brief me on what to do. I don't want to embarrass you."

"Good grief, Chelsea, I'm afraid I'll be the one to make the mistakes. Although I've studied a lot about Japanese culture, I've never experienced a tea ceremony. Don't know how long hers will take. Some last four hours and you have to kneel the whole time. This afternoon I had trouble with my knees after fifteen minutes."

"We'll do our best. I don't care if my knees crack open. For your family's honor, I vow to kneel for as long as necessary and I bet you will too."

"Okay, let's drink to that," he cried, refilling their cups.

As the evening wore on, they grew more relaxed—eating, drinking sake, Chelsea talking about San Francisco—the parrots on Telegraph Hill, the crazies on Market Street—Yoshi talking about a family of jugglers from Port Townsend and the time he was on a ferryboat that ran aground. Lots of laughter.

The little Japanese lady came back, removed their dinner trays and brought them gingered pears and tea.

After the woman left, Chelsea found herself saying, "Creating a relationship is like walking a tightrope."

He stared into his small bowl of pears and slowly nodded. "First steps are the hardest."

"And if you get out in the middle and fall off...."

"Better not be high in the air," he finished with a chuckle.

She laughed and met his eyes. "I think both of us are pretty well grounded."

As they drank the tea and ate the pears, she told him about Eric and her concerns about being here.

"It does sound peculiar," Yoshi agreed. "You need answers from your boyfriend."

"I know. Sometimes he's not open with me. You'd think by now I'd know more about him, but I don't. He's pretty closed-mouth about what he does." She met his eyes. "Do you have a girlfriend?"

"Not now. I did have a long-term relationship with a lady by the name of Evelyn. Last year, though, it grew strained after she met a guy online and got into perpetual texting with him. I scarcely see her any more."

They agreed life could be a lonely place, worse though if you had a relationship with a person who hid his thoughts or tried to manipulate your life. Several times, in moments of complete agreement, they briefly clasped hands across the table.

Finally, Chelsea said, "I'm getting sleepy. Too much sightseeing." She stood up and stretched.

He scrambled to his feet. "I'll see you back to your room."

She opened the garden screen. "No need. I'm only three rooms down. Besides, look, there's a three quarter moon to help me find my way. Thanks for the wonderful evening."

He smiled. "My pleasure. Don't know when I've enjoyed a dinner more. Until tomorrow at ten, then."

"Yes, in front of the inn." She slipped into her zori, blew him a kiss and left.

CHAPTER 8

The shoji screen to her room was partially open. Had she left it that way? No. She remembered shutting it. Odd.

Depositing her zori on the landing, she stepped inside. It was too dark to see. She stood there, sensing something wrong. Should she leave? Go back outside?

Just my imagination, she concluded. So many uncertainties lately.

Carefully, she moved toward the low table, not wanting to fall into the pit beneath it. Her eyes adjusted. The table wasn't there, the pit covered, a futon spread over it. This must be the usual setup: living room by day, bedroom by night. Next to the futon was the unlit lantern. As she reached to turn it on, a hand grasped her wrist.

She fell to her knees with a gasp.

A gruff male voice said, "No light, please."

Before she could scream, another hand clapped over her mouth.

"Quiet!" commanded the voice.

She froze.

He released her hand and mouth. "I am not here to harm you."

She recognized the voice—Kagawa, her guide. "What do you want?" she sputtered, scrambling to her feet

"My job is to protect your briefcase," he said. "You went away and left it behind. Now you have returned, I shall leave. I trust I did not alarm you."

"You alarmed me a great deal and you know it." Her anger rose. "Look, Kagawa, I don't need your protection. In the future, I'll haul my briefcase every place I go. Will that please you and your boss?"

"Yes."

"Then keep your distance."

He bowed and left through the shoji to the hall, closing it behind him.

Trembling, she sank down onto the tatami, still feeling Kagawa's hand over her mouth, his other hand on her wrist, hands that gave her the creeps, both missing their little fingers.

He had met her this morning at the Tokyo Train Station, where she was scheduled to take the Bullet Train for her two nights in Kyoto. As she emerged from Mr. Tamiyasu's limousine, he stood before her, red flower in his buttonhole, legs spread apart as if he getting ready to ram through a door.

"I am Kagawa," he had informed her in a voice that sounded like a file pulled over sandpaper. "From here on I am your guide. Hold your briefcase close to your chest. These days thieves are common." He removed her suitcase from the trunk and led her to the Bullet Train through a maze of stairways. All the way to Kyoto, Kagawa sat across the aisle and watched her.

At first it had disturbed Chelsea that Mr. Hayashi had arranged for such a terrible man to be her guide. But after today's whirlwind tour through Kyoto during which Kagawa dispensed knowledgeable details about temples and shrines and found ways to circumvent tourist lines, she could see why Mr. Hayashi had picked him for the job. Now, she realized it was also for another reason.

She crawled over and switched on the lantern. The low table was against the wall; the top of the futon cover had been folded back in an inviting manner. Through the half-open shoji she saw the moonlit garden bathed in a silvery light.

Like a beautiful painting, she thought, rising and going to the doorway for a closer view. But those shadows...is someone hiding behind the pines? No, no, I'm jumpy, seeing things that don't exist.

She closed the garden shoji and wished she could lock it.

Deciding to make certain the envelope was still in her briefcase, she slid back the closet shoji, opened her case, and drew it out. No name on on the front. No address. On the back, only the unbroken red seal.

Yoshi might know what the peony meant. He might know something about Hayashi. Might have an idea what could be valuable enough to hide in a wax-sealed envelope and placed under guard until sent to San Francisco with a carrier.

But what if Kagawa wouldn't allow Yoshi to come with her tomorrow? Did she have to be protected from all outsiders? Was this envelope so valuable, other people would try to steal it?

Her eyes narrowed. Maybe even Yoshi? This afternoon, he was the one who made the initial contact with her. Could she trust him? What was going on here?

Pulling out her cell phone, she punched in Eric's private number, the one she always used. She would insist he tell her what was in the envelope. No way she would carry onto a plane something illegal or dangerous, even if Eric begged her in his most charming manner.

Again she got Eric's voice mail.

She grit her teeth. Must be screening his calls. Doesn't want to talk to me. Hasn't returned my messages. What's with this guy?

She barked into the receiver, "Eric, call me by tomorrow afternoon. Why the hell is this envelope so important? I don't like what's happening over here. You got me into a mess. Call me, damn you."

A hollow clacking sound startled her, growing louder, ceasing, starting again, moving closer. Catching her breath, she slipped the envelope into her case, shoved it into the closet and slid the shoji across. She stood there protectively, her back to the closet.

Again the clacking. It reminded her of sounds made when a train ran across a wooden bridge. Sounds from her childhood, heard at night in the little apartment above her parents grocery store. Sounds that frightened her for it seemed the train would crash through the window and run over her. She listened intently, a cold chill creeping over her.

Darkness edged across the garden side of her shoji, the moonlight gradually disappearing.

She caught her breath and drew back closer to the closet.

All of the outside scene was gone now.

The sounds were repeated for the next room down, and on and on. Then, along the side of the inn. Now they seemed to be moving across the front of the building. Was the entire inn being wrapped up? Why?

She darted to the garden shoji, cautiously opened it a few inches and touched what had caused the darkness. Wooden panels.

I'm closed off from the world, she told herself, feeling her blood pressure rise. I'm sealed in. Even the words bothered her—s*ealed in*. The thought rang another alarm. Kagawa is in the inn with me.

CHAPTER 9

Yoshi awoke at eight in the morning to the sound of the outside shutters being drawn back. A nice alarm clock, he thought.

The rhythmical clacking continued along the side of the inn as the shutters were opened. Yoshi imagined a member of the kabuki playing a pair of wooden sticks. He half expected to hear a chanting voice accompany the sounds, imagined a group of actors in the garden, moving with precise, measured steps, their faces and gestures ordained from the past.

He knew about the ancient custom of shuttering inns against inclement weather and to guard against thieves and assassins, but he hadn't realized the custom was still practiced. Probably only at the old places, he concluded.

Slipping out of his warm futon covers, he put on his yukata and then slid open the garden shoji. Sunlight poured into the room. The air smelled of wet pine needles and fragrant wood. He stepped out onto the landing and saw a young Japanese man pulling the shutters back on other rooms down the line. There was Chelsea's room.

A warm glow swept through him. "I'm only 33," she had laughingly said last night after finding out he was 38. Amazing how such a young lady could be a partner in a law firm. "Just a small firm of twelve lawyers," she had told him, but still her associates must have considered her a great asset.

He examined his set of shutters, now folded back into a tall, well-crafted enclosure. Fine wood, oiled, obviously old but in good condition. Once again he glanced toward Chelsea's room. He felt the same desire to jump around as before a tennis match. He broke into a series of knee bends, then jogged in place. *Off to Nara at ten*, he felt like shouting at the sky. *I'm going to Nara with a lovely lady.*

Good grief, he cautioned himself. So what if he was spending the day with a beautiful, fascinating, intelligent woman. It wouldn't do to get carried away. Mistakes happen when emotions cloud judgments. Glancing at his watch, he realized breakfast would come in twenty minutes. Barely time to shave and dress.

He hurried inside, shut the garden shoji and pulled open the hall shoji. His bathroom was behind another screen to the right, the one ahead leading directly into the inn's office and public areas. So many identical looking shojis, it took a while after his first arrival to remember which led where. Was his shaving kit in here? Yes, on the ledge by the sink. Get busy, he told himself.

When he returned to his room, the futon was gone, the pit open, the table in the center as before, cushioned seat ready for him. The ladies of the inn at work again. Quiet, efficient, knowing the correct time to enter his room, do what must be done and disappear like ghosts.

He decided to wear his suit. This was a special day. Jeans seemed inconsiderate, denying the importance of the occasion. Yesterday he had thought his suit a mistake at Grandmother's house. On second thought, even though he found it uncomfortable to kneel, to maneuver about on the lily pad pillow, he had shown Grandmother respect by appearing in a more formal manner. Surely that much had been a good idea.

Hurriedly, he dressed, fumbling with his shirt buttons. He opened the shoji to the garden and took deep breaths to calm down.

"*Gomen nasai,*" called a familiar voice from the other side of the hallway shoji.

It was breakfast, arriving the moment he finished with his tie. Did the little lady have x-ray vision? Was it a matter of experience, a tuning in to needs, the business of politeness extended into service? The end result, perhaps its purpose, to iron out life's wrinkles? Or were people in the inn watching him, for some reason keeping their eyes on everything he did?

Breakfast was a shorthand version of dinner: soup, rice, tsukemono, egg custard, and a nutty-flavored tea. Genmai cha, he suspected. Delicious. He wished for more time to enjoy it.

A minute before ten, he walked out into the hallway. Chelsea was waiting by the front desk. "How come you brought your briefcase?" he asked her.

"Important papers," she answered, avoiding his eyes.

Her voice was cautious, her bearing stiff. Last night's sweetness gone. Had the briefcase affected her personality? Maybe it was the hat.

His excitement dwindled away. He felt like excusing himself, saying he had forgotten a previous engagement, turning around and slipping back into his room. Courage, he commanded himself. Somewhere was the Chelsea of yesterday. If he persevered, he would find her again.

In the inn's foyer stood the old man, the keeper of the shoes. He bowed, the top of his bald head looking like a peeled peach. In an instant he produced their shoes. While they sat on the bench to put them on, the old man dropped their discarded slippers in what appeared to be a laundry basket, and then moved back a respectful distance, his head lowered so the peeled peach glowed in the morning sunlight.

Yoshi wondered if the old man knew him more by his feet than his face. Each time Yoshi entered the inn, the old man took his shoes as if accepting a present, carefully placed them in a row with many other pairs, and, without pause, produced the correct size of slippers for him to wear inside. His job, small as it was, executed with pride.

Chelsea's driver was dressed in a dark blue suit and striped tie, incongruous with his coarse features and prize-fighter build. He stood beside a black limousine. As they approached, the driver's frown deepened. "Excuse me, but who is this?" he said glaring at Yoshi.

"My American friend," Chelsea said curtly. "I've invited him to go with us."

Kagawa growled, "I am supposed to carry only one passenger—you, Miss Jarvis."

Yoshi said quickly, "I'll pay for any extra cost."

"It is not a matter of money," Kagawa grunted, jaw protruding. "It is a matter of my orders. Please, inform me who you are."

"Yoshi Moore."

Kagawa inclined his head slightly, his eyes still on Yoshi. "Sorry, but I must know where you live, what your work is, what business you have in Japan and why you wish to go to Nara with Miss Jarvis."

Yoshi stiffened. "I am a university professor from the State of Washington." He raised his chin. "And my business in Japan is none of yours. Neither is my reason for going to Nara with Miss Jarvis."

Another grunt from Kagawa. He rubbed his mouth and chin and continued to inspect Yoshi.

"Enough of this!" Chelsea said, her laugh unmirthful. "Come on, Yoshi."

She grasped the car door handle, but Kagawa's hand clamped over hers, the stub of his little finger protruding grotesquely.

Yoshi blinked. He glanced at the driver's other hand. Both little fingers missing. He noted the limousine was a black Cadillac. Dark windows hid the interior. It all fit. He swallowed hard. Did Chelsea know this fellow's connections?

Kagawa forced her fingers free.

Chelsea stepped back, anger on her face.

Kagawa spoke in a steely voice. "Why do you wish this man to go with us?"

She drew herself up, the hat giving her a good three inches over the muscular man. "Because he is my friend," she announced belligerently.

Yoshi found himself shouting, "Don't interfere with us." He straightened his back. "I intend to travel to Nara with Miss Jarvis. If you won't take us I shall call a taxi." Although he realized there was no way of intimidating this thug, he hoped his blast would gain Chelsea's respect.

The three stood in a circle, staring at each other.

"Kagawa-san," Chelsea said in a conciliatory manner, "I am certain you know everything about Nara. And since your English is excellent, I know you will produce lucid explanations. However, to be frank, and at this time I feel it necessary to be frank, your harsh manner does not give me an ounce of enjoyment. Should you make my day miserable, I doubt if Mr. Hayashi will be"—she paused and emphasized the next word—"pleased with you." A bland smile, a softer voice. "May we proceed now?"

Kagawa's face wrinkled into the fierce look of a deva king guarding a temple gate. He pulled on a pair of white gloves.

The three continued to stand there, silently eyeing each other.

Finally, Kagawa nodded and took her briefcase. Stepping aside, he opened the back door and bowed low.

Chelsea and Yoshi climbed into the car.

CHAPTER 10

After the door closed, Yoshi whispered in Chelsea's ear, "He's yakuza."

She raised her eyebrows. "What?"

"Yakuza."

"Yakuza?"

"Sh-h-h. Japanese Mafia." He pointed to the partition and said in a conversational voice. "These partitions are supposed to give back seat privacy, but I bet our driver can hear everything we have to say."

"Most likely," she replied and inched closer to Yoshi, grasping his arm.

A roar built up in Yoshi's ears, like thunder coming closer—tension from the situation with Kagawa, the warmth of her body against him. Relax, he told himself.

A loud snap startled him.

Chelsea let go of his arm.

He glanced around the interior. The sound came from all four doors. Gingerly, he tried his door handle. Locked. The car moved, but he heard no engine. A soundproofed interior. He exchanged a look with Chelsea.

She straightened her hat. "The limousine in Tokyo had no handles," she said as if this was some improvement.

From the speakers floated haunting notes of a Japanese flute punctuated by sharp drum beats. Cool air rushed in from the vents. Yoshi shivered. Immediately, the air turned warm.

No doubt the thug would notice everything, Yoshi concluded. Well, so would he. If necessary, he would battle the goon. Just how, he had no idea, but he would find a way.

Chelsea fished a small guide book from her skirt pocket. For the approximate hour of the drive, she poured over the pages about Nara, reading to Yoshi details about the Todaiji Temple that housed the colossal bronze Buddha. About the Kasuga Shrine and its road lined with stone lanterns, lit during celebrations. About the tame deer that roamed the park. About other temples and shrines, pagodas, ponds and gates.

Yoshi assessed it all. Meanwhile, from the perimeter of his vision, he kept track of Kagawa, who concentrated on the road, only an occasional glance back at them.

In Nara, Kagawa parked on a lot already crowded with automobiles. The door locks clicked open. Ceremoniously, the driver opened the back door on Chelsea's side, bowing to each as they emerged.

"First we visit the Todaiji Temple," Kagawa announced. He retrieved Chelsea's briefcase from the trunk and locked the limousine. "Since you just read about the temple, no need for me to repeat details." He smirked.

Chelsea and Yoshi exchanged knowing looks.

"Later we visit Deer Park," Kagawa continued. "You also read about that place, so I see no necessity of repeating information." Another smirk. "Your guide book was quite lucid." He led the way, elbows angled out, chin jutting forward, no movement to his upper body, the briefcase held waist high, gloves still on.

From the back, Kagawa reminded Yoshi of an English butler. Why didn't he leave the briefcase in the car? he wondered. *Yakuza. Yakuza.* The word kept flashing across his mind like a warning signal. How did this man get to be Chelsea's guide?

They followed him toward a monumental gate supported by eighteen pillars. In its exterior niches stood a pair of wooden figures—guards or warriors—of giant proportions, at least three times the size of ordinary men.

As Yoshi walked past the wooden figures, their eyes seemed to focus down on him. Deciding he was getting too paranoid, he made an effort to lighten up. Amusing the way Kagawa carried her briefcase. Funny how Chelsea continually eyed the case as if it might explode. A comic scene—he and Chelsea striding across a temple courtyard behind a weird-looking gangster who bore a briefcase as if it were an offering.

Outside the Hall of the Great Buddha, Yoshi and Chelsea paused to inspect a large, intricately wrought lantern on a pedestal. A Japanese man with thick lips and dark glasses appeared beside Kagawa. It was obvious they knew each other. Arms folded, the two men quietly conversed, the thick-lipped man periodically staring at Yoshi.

"I don't like the looks of that guy," Chelsea muttered to Yoshi.

"I dislike them both," he replied softly.

They walked past the men, up the stairs toward the doorway of the Main Hall.

Glancing back, Yoshi noted the two men were walking toward the stairs, their eyes focused on him. He took Chelsea's arm and quickened his steps.

It was dim and cool inside, crowded with people who spoke in hushed tones. He peered up at the bronze statue. It was a technical tour de force, the Great Buddha, the Daibutsu, the most gigantic human form he had ever seen. He remembered the details Chelsea had read to him: 53.5 feet tall, sitting cross-legged on fifty-six bronze lotus petals, each ten feet high, supported by a massive stone foundation seven feet in height. Details were always easy for Yoshi to remember. But, hearing her read about the Great Buddha had not prepared him for its sight. Never had he seen such a huge figure, mysterious yet peaceful.

Another time came to his mind—a trip in the Cascades, camping out with his father. He woke up in the middle of the night and stared up at a billion stars, face to face with his insignificance, feeling close to a cosmic understanding. He had a similar feeling as he gazed at the gigantic bronze statue. Not that he thought the statue was beautiful. Its proportions looked off. It was its size, the incomprehensibility of how such an enormous bronze figure could be created, the immensity of it that filled him with awe.

The gentle pressure of Chelsea's hand on his shoulder brought him back to the present. He smiled, she smiled back, and somehow he knew she understood what he felt.

Yoshi noted Kagawa entering the temple doorway with the big-lipped man. "Let's go this way," he said to Chelsea and edged past a large tour group, hoping to find a less crowded area where he could speak with her privately. The left corner of the Hall, behind the Daibutsu, was empty of people. He stopped near an odd-looking wooden statue about 18 feet in height, a figure that appeared to be trampling a demon.

"Chelsea," he said softly, "why did you come to Japan?"

She looked away, perspiration on her forehead and upper lip. "We should go back where Kagawa can see us."

"Why?"

"So he won't think we're trying to run away. She pressed her lips together, as if assessing how much to tell.

"Is there a reason we might want to run?"

"Yes, perhaps. Well, maybe. I mean, I think so." She grabbed his arms. "Yoshi, I wish I had never come. Weird things are happening. I—I was sent to Tokyo to negotiate a contract."

"Who sent you?"

"A client."

"Someone you can trust?"

"I thought so, but now, I'm not sure."

"A friend? A relative? Someone you know well?"

She stepped back. "In my business," she said tightly, "I'm the one who asks questions."

"Look, Chelsea, I have a strong reason to believe both men are yakuza. You're dealing, we're both dealing, with gangsters. Does it matter which one of us asks the questions?"

She stared at him for a moment, then nodded. "Okay." Assuming a business-like tone, she said, "My client is Eric Hunter. I told you about him last night. I've known him for a year, known him quite well." She swallowed hard and glanced around, not meeting Yoshi's eyes. "He owns a respectable Asian travel agency in San Francisco. Hardly the gangster type." She wiped the perspiration from her upper lip. "Because of his agency, he often visits Japan to arrange tours, and, well, he used to live in Tokyo, but I can't imagine...." Her voice faded.

"Who did he send you to see?"

"Mr. Hayashi, the head of a Tokyo corporation. An investment company who needed travel arrangements for its employees. That's what he said." Her eyes met his. "Does the yakuza have a symbol, a red flower?"

"The yakuza isn't just one group. It's composed of separate syndicates, each divided into gangs. A gang could have a symbol." His eyes narrowed. "What kind of red flower?"

"A peony."

Across Yoshi's mind flashed a picture of his Grandmother's garden. "Peonies grow all over Japan," he said. "Where have you seen this symbol?"

"In the buttonholes of certain men who met me in Tokyo, on a china tea set in an office, in a bowl on a desk. Yesterday, I was given a manila envelope sealed with a blob of red wax imprinted with a peony. I have no idea what's in the envelope, but I'm supposed to take it back to the States and deliver it to Eric."

"Is the envelope in your briefcase?"

"Yes, along with the contract I was sent here to negotiate, only there wasn't much need for—"

From around the side of the statue, her briefcase appeared. "Kagawa's coming," she whispered. "He'll think we're hiding from him."

Before he could even think about what he was doing, Yoshi took her in his arms and kissed her.

She kissed him back with more emotion than he had counted on. He found himself deeply involved. He wanted to pick Chelsea up, rush off to a hidden corner and make passionate love.

He released her, and backed away, took several deep breaths and muttered, "It's all right, he's gone now."

"Who's gone?" she asked, her hat askew.

"Kagawa."

"Oh."

"Now he knows why we're hiding."

"I see." She straightened her hat.

"Sorry I grabbed you like that and, well, you know. I don't want you to think I'm the kind of fellow who...." He decided to give up trying to explain. The gleam in her eyes surprised him. He felt like a man who had just received a hot tip on a race. He reached out and took her hand.

She gave his a quick squeeze.

They moved around the Great Buddha and met Kagawa, a ferocious frown on his face. Yoshi bowed and said, "Greetings, Kagawa-san. Where do we go next?"

"Much to see," Kagawa rumbled.

They marched down the steps, three abreast, Chelsea in the middle, incoming tourists parting as if they were a military contingent.

The thick-lipped man with dark glasses was nowhere to be seen.

CHAPTER 11

Kagawa established a rigid procedure. He drove them to a temple, parked and led them on a ten-minute tour, walked them back to the limousine and drove on to a garden, repeating the procedure. More temples. More gardens. Each had its time limit.

Yoshi tried to concentrate on architecture and settings. He examined the Five-Storied Pagoda, the carving of Shaka-Nyorai, the Sarusawa Pond, some shrines that seemed all the same, Deer Park. He stared at blossoming cherry trees and groves of cedars. In an animated fashion he chatted with Chelsea, only half conscious of what he said. He could hear his heart thumping. Disaster seemed close. He felt on the edge of a deep pit.

It wasn't only his fear of what Kagawa might do. It was his frightful longing to kiss Chelsea again, the remembered feel of her soft body when he held her in his arms. He took deep breaths, blowing out each one slower than the last, all the while pretending to examine the sights of Nara and chatting about them with Chelsea. What would she say if she knew his desire was to carry her off to a flower-filled room and make passionate love? Would she think him insane? Careful, Yoshi, careful, he warned himself, new ground here.

In spite of his feelings about Chelsea, Yoshi did not lose track of Kagawa, peering at him around edges of windows, doors, statues, buildings. Ah, there he is—Kagawa, the ghoul, on the steps, beside the bench, leaning against the tree, the briefcase always with him.

It was just after a tame deer came up to them that the thick-lipped man with dark glasses reappeared. Arms folded, he conversed with Kagawa, their heads close together, both eyeing Yoshi. Again his heart thumped, even louder.

Now the thick-lipped man followed them everywhere: driving in another limousine, walking where they walked, always keeping about ten feet away—the same distance behind them as Kagawa walked ahead.

Once Chelsea stopped and glared back at him. The man stopped and lit a cigarette. He blew a stream of smoke toward her. She called to Kagawa, "Who's the obnoxious guy following us?"

"My friend," he called back.

"Tell him to go away."

Kagawa continued walking, saying nothing.

Yoshi shouted, "Miss Jarvis and I consider your friend annoying."

"I am sorry," Kagawa said over his shoulder. "It is necessary for him to be with us."

They walked on in silence, Kagawa still holding the briefcase in front of him, although not as high as before.

At two o'clock, Chelsea said to Kagawa, "May we go somewhere for lunch or do we continue to look at sights until we pass out?"

Kagawa didn't answer. However, he cut his tour of the stone lantern path to five minutes and led them back to the limousine. Then he drove them to a noodle stand on a small lane off the main street. A three-sectioned banner hung above the entrance, the door wide open. Inside, a man sat on one of the five bamboo stools at the counter. Upon seeing the intruders, he hurriedly finished his bowl of noodles and left.

Yoshi wondered if the appearance of Kagawa had bothered the fellow. Or was it the sight of Chelsea, this tall, beautiful, Caucasian woman in the peculiar black hat who walked with such graceful authority. On their morning tour Yoshi had been aware of numerous heads turning to gaze at her as she passed. Even he, taller than most of the Japanese people, had drawn a few looks.

In back of the counter, a thin, hollow-cheeked man appeared from behind a navy blue curtain that partly covered a doorway. While he scrutinized them, he continually wiped his hands on his apron.

Yoshi chose the end stool; Chelsea sat next to him; Kagawa remained at the entrance. Trying to make his voice sound casual, Yoshi said, "Chelsea, what would you like to eat?"

"I'd love a cheeseburger, French fries and a coke, but I'll settle for noodles—any kind."

"*Nabeyaki udon o kudasai,*" Yoshi informed the man. "*Futatsu.*" He held up two fingers in case his pronunciation was off.

"*Hai,*" the man replied as if he'd received an electric shock. He plunged into the back room, the curtain snapping inward after him.

Six minutes later, the man returned with chopsticks and two steaming bowls: noodles in broth, with squares of chicken, mushrooms and other vegetables, topped with an egg, cooked by the hot liquid beneath. His service complete, the man disappeared behind the blue curtain.

They ate in silence, chopsticks now and then clicking against the sides of the bowls. Periodically, Yoshi glanced back at Kagawa, still by the front doorway, the expression on his face like a carved demon. Although Chelsea seemed to enjoy her noodles, Yoshi noted she occasionally peered furtively over her shoulder.

When finished, Yoshi brought out his wallet and called towards the kitchen, "*Ikura desuka?*"

The proprietor stepped out, glanced at Kagawa, then shook his head at Yoshi, waving the wallet away. "*Muryo,*" he said, his head respectfully inclined.

"What did he say?" whispered Chelsea.

"We don't need to pay," Yoshi whispered back. "For some reason our meals were free." He replaced his wallet. "*Arigato,*" he thanked the man, who nodded.

Chelsea spun around on the stool. "Kagawa-san, I'm sick of this tour." She straightened her hat and rose as if ready to do battle. "Take us back to the inn."

"I have another temple to show you," Kagawa said darkly.

"I don't care. I'm all templed out and I've got a headache." She slipped past his bulky form and into the street.

"Besides," added Yoshi, starting to follow, "we have an appointment at four."

Kagawa stood in front of him. He grunted, "What appointment?"

"Let me through the doorway?"

Kagawa didn't move. "What appointment?" he repeated, emphasizing each word.

Chelsea shouted from the street. "None of your damned business."

Kagawa's head whipped toward her.

Yoshi attempted to duck by Kagawa's arm, but couldn't make the maneuver as Kagawa had lowered his arm, closing off the space.

Facing Yoshi, Kagawa said in a low, deadly voice, "Miss Jarvis goes nowhere unless I go with her."

Yoshi heard a rustle behind him. Glancing back, he saw the dark blue curtain swaying, the proprietor gone.

"See here," Yoshi said firmly, "I demand you step aside."

"I repeat," Kagawa growled, "Miss Jarvis goes no place alone with you,"

Yoshi pushed at Kagawa, trying to force his way outside. The thug must be made of stone, he thought, or else he's welded to the door. "She certainly will come with me," he bellowed.

"No!" The word exploded from Kagawa. He shoved Yoshi back.

Yoshi staggered, grasping a stool to keep from falling. Angry now, he lowered his head with the notion of using it as a battering ram.

Kagawa shouted something in Japanese.

Before Yoshi could step forward, an arm encircled him from behind, a hand slapped over his mouth. He struggled, but couldn't move. Kagawa vanished. Frantically Yoshi tried to get loose. Tried to bite the hand over his mouth. Tried to kick whoever held his arms. He heard the limousine door slam, the engine rev, the vehicle drive away. He struggled harder.

Abruptly, his assailant released him.

Whirling around, Yoshi confronted his attacker—the thick-lipped man in dark glasses. Calmly, the man lit a cigarette.

"You bastard!" Yoshi shrieked at him. He ran outside, yelling for Chelsea, although he knew she wouldn't be there. He raced down the narrow lane. There still might be time to catch the limousine if it stopped for traffic on the main street. As he ran, he shouted her name over and over. Two little girls playing ball, flattened against a building, terror on their faces. When Yoshi reached the main street, he searched the lines of cars that streamed past in each direction. The black limousine was gone.

My fault, he chided himself, my fault. I should have slipped out when she did, should have held on to her hand, kept her with me, never should have mentioned our four o'clock appointment.

A sudden fury seized him. He would go back to the restaurant and wring the neck of the thick-lipped man. He charged back down the narrow lane, feeling stronger than a bull entering a ring.

Again the two girls clutched their ball and watched him pass as if he were a devil on the loose.

The noodle stand was closed. He tried the door handle. Locked. He banged on the door. No answer. He bellowed for the proprietor. Banged some more. All his vengeance concentrated on this wooden obstacle.

How long he stayed at that door, he had no idea, but sometime later he looked toward the main thoroughfare and noticed a group of people gathered at the corner.

There they stood—four men and two women, one in a kimono—peering down the narrow lane, observing Yoshi as if he were an enemy who had penetrated their world. The two little girls were gone. He supposed they had fled to tell their mothers about the crazy man.

Yoshi slowly walked toward the people, his arms raised as if they held a gun on him. The two women scurried away. "*Sumimasen,*" Yoshi called to the men. "*Shitsurei shimashita. Gomen nasai.*" Again and again he begged forgiveness for being so rude.

When he reached the street, one of the men, his face shaped like an almond, politely asked in Japanese if he could be of any assistance. "*Hai,*" Yoshi replied wearily. In halting Japanese, hoping his words were right, disturbed at his incompetence with the language, he asked if someone could please show him the way to the train station. He tried to explain how he had lost a dear friend and how upsetting this was to him and how he must go back to Kyoto to save her from serious difficulties. They listened and nodded, and he wondered if they understood.

The almond-faced man led him to the railway station and waited, saying he wished to make certain Yoshi boarded the right train.

No seats were available. The train was crowded. When Yoshi peered out the window and waved goodbye, the man stood on the platform, feet together, hands to his side, executing a proper bow.

Yoshi wondered if the man had helped him just to eliminate the disturbing person who had frightened his friends. Or did he believe to help a man in distress was the honorable thing to do? No way of knowing. No way of knowing what anyone in Japan thought about him.

Never had he felt so out of place, so lost, so frightened. How was he going to find Chelsea? Where had Kagawa taken her? Was she all right? Maybe he'd never see her again.

Calm down, Yoshi told himself. Think this through. First he would talk to the ladies at the inn. The train started up and he grasped one of the leather straps above him for balance. Surely the people at the inn would help him. He pursed his lips. Unless they were under the wing of the yakuza.

CHAPTER 12

As the limousine sped away from the noodle stand, Chelsea pounded on the window glass and shouted for help. Two girls playing ball on the narrow street paid no attention.

They can't see through this glass, she remembered, and the car is soundproof. In frustration, she snatched off her high-heel shoes and beat a tattoo on the partition between front and back seats. Music poured from the speakers—diabolic Wagner.

Realizing the futility of getting Kagawa's attention, she put her shoes back on, yanked off her bowler, swept back her damp bangs and wiped her forehead on the sleeve of her jacket. Jamming on her hat, she leaned back, arms folded, and glowered at the back of Kagawa's head as if her eyes could drill holes through his brain.

He navigated on, smoothly, mechanically, saying nothing. He's a damned robotic monster, she thought, the way he had shoved her into his limousine, slammed the door, snapped the locks and drove off, leaving Yoshi behind, stranded at the noodle stand.

The music continued to blare. The streets of Nara fled past, a blur of black and white cars and empty faces against a backdrop of unreadable signs and a jumble of buildings. She felt trapped in a video but not part of the scene, as if she'd been squeezed into the camera.

Kagawa had abducted her right after Yoshi told him about their four o'clock appointment. Obviously, Kagawa thought that must not happen. All because she would be away from his control. She and the manila envelope must be together, Kagawa as their guard at all times. Ha! She would show him. She would find a way to get back her briefcase, whip out Hayashi's manila envelope and rip it open. To hell with it being a sealed document in a client/attorney relationship. Hayashi was no longer her client. He was a criminal who might be involving her in a criminal act.

Yes, time for disclosure. Time to tear open the damned thing. See what was inside. Jot down pertinent information. Get a handle on everything. After that, ditch Kagawa and find Yoshi.

Why was it important to find Yoshi? she asked herself. Because she liked him, she concluded. Enjoyed his company. Besides, no way she could move about in this country on her own, what with the language barrier and her non-Asian looks. Yoshi spoke Japanese, could pass for a Japanese person, even if only half so. He could front for her while she hid in a remote village, away from these creeps who dictated her every move. She'd lie low for a week, then return to the States in a circuitous manner. Surely Yoshi wouldn't let her down.

She yanked her cell phone from her pocket, then remembered she didn't have Yoshi's number. Even if she had it, she realized this wouldn't be a good time to call him. Kagawa would hear everything she said. But she could text Yoshi, although she considered it unlikely a staid English professor did that sort of thing. She sighed. He might not even have a cell phone.

What good was it to think of those possibilities. She had no number for Yoshi. Period! She shoved her phone back in her pocket, but kept one hand on it.

Where was Kagawa taking her? Maybe he would dump her in some secret place, tie her up and leave her there until Hayashi decided what to do with her. No, surely not that.

It makes more sense for Kagawa to take me back to the inn, she concluded. Why? Because they need my help. They want me to carry the letter to San Francisco. The minute I get back to the room, I'll cancel tomorrow's flight so my ticket will still be good; ask McCloskey to postpone the Thompson trial; tell Vera to reschedule all appointments. Everything at the office can be managed.

Carefully she pulled out her phone. Since Eric obviously had no intention of returning her other three messages she decided to text him. She typed in Eric's e-mail address and then tapped *Go to hell!*

There, she felt better. When she returned to San Francisco, she would have no more contact with the toad. To think she had trusted him, believed in him, slept with him. Cared about him, for God's sake. The jerk could take his sweet words, his good looks, his clever, funny ways and lay them on some other unsuspecting female. She would report him to the D.A.

No, best to extricate myself gradually. When he asks for the manila envelope I'll say, "Oh, hasn't it come yet? I mailed it to you. Can't imagine why you haven't received it. Hope nothing too important was inside." She wrinkled her nose, wishing she hadn't sent that text message, played dumb instead.

Damn Eric Hunter.

Her eyes watered. I'm not crying, she told herself, squeezing her eyes shut, It's been a long, tough day. I'm just tired.

However, she was crying. She had believed in Eric, cared about him, counted on him too heavily. He had wounded her, and it wasn't a wound she accepted lightly.

They reached the inn quickly. The moment the limousine locks clicked open, she leaped out and grabbed her briefcase from a startled Kagawa, who was just getting out of the driver's seat. She fled inside, tossing her heels into the foyer and snatching a pair of slippers from the surprised shoe-keeper.

On the low table in her room, the steaming teapot and porcelain cup looked inviting. Comforting. Her throat felt sandpapered. She was thirsty. After tossing her briefcase into the closet, she knelt by the table, poured a cup and then consumed it, the temperature of the liquid just right. She poured another cup. Drank that.

Then she noticed Kagawa, standing beside her. He looked fuzzy, bathed in a pale, feathery light. Blinking, she tried to keep him from fading away, tried to keep everything from fading, clutched the table and tried so hard to focus.

The tea, she thought in desperation. Oh, my God, I've been drugged.

CHAPTER 13

The train speeded up. Yoshi clutched the overhead strap tighter and closed his eyes to block out the throng of Japanese who pressed in around him as tightly as dried figs in a box. He felt self-conscious, not because he was touching bodies, but because his head jutted up higher. He stood there, determined to be calm, eyes closed, in limbo, slightly swaying with the motion of the train. For some unknown reason he thought about the second stanza of "Ode on a Grecian Urn. "Silently he mouthed the words:

> *Heard melodies are sweet, but those unheard*
> *Are sweeter; therefore, ye soft pipes, play on;*
> *Not to the sensual ear, but, more endear'd*
> *Pipe to the spirit ditties of no tone:*
> *Fair youth, beneath the trees, thou canst not leave*
> *Thy son, nor ever can those trees be bare;*
> *Bold Lover, never, never canst thou kiss,*
> *Though winning near the goal—yet, do not grieve;*
> *She cannot fade, though thou hast not thy bliss,*
> *For ever wilt thou love, and she be fair!*

Did those lines remind him of Chelsea because he wanted to maintain a beautiful, perfect picture of her? In his mind he saw her by the maple tree in the Momiji-ya garden, dressed in the inn's pale green yukata, her pearl earrings aglow, a leaf held in her hand. In the Todaiji Temple of Nara, again he saw her wearing the pale green yukata. He held her in his arms, her body soft and warm beneath the loose garment.

He opened his eyes. No! In the temple she wore a tailored suit and a bowler hat. But it seemed too difficult to remember Chelsea that way. He couldn't imagine her marching into a courtroom and arguing a case before a judge. Or confronting gangsters.

Why not?

I want her to need me, he answered himself.

He squeezed his eyelids shut again and wished he knew nothing about the yakuza, wished he had not come with Chelsea to Nara. If he had closed the glass doors yesterday, if he hadn't stepped into the garden, his lovely vision of her would have remained in tact, and most likely she would be safe now, for he was the cause of her difficulties with that thug, Kagawa.

Yet, he *had* stepped out. Now, as he stood on the train, packed in tightly, swaying with the crowd, her realities tumbled back in on him. He thought hard and found he could picture her operating in different roles: the fragile beauty in the garden, the playful friend at dinner, the intelligent companion, the capable lawyer, the tender woman in his arms. All of these aspects of Chelsea might fit together in his mind if he let them. The idea that they could, interested him, although he wasn't sure he was ready to face a Chelsea of such multi dimensions. What frightened him most were his obsessive feelings about her—a woman he had known less than 24 hours.

How he felt now was a revealing experience. For so long he had maintained a controlled distance from people that his world had become encased in unreality. Time to break out, he thought. Let filtered visions float away.

Panic hit him. He opened his eyes and gazed wildly over the sea of heads. What if he never saw Chelsea again? Where had Kagawa taken her? He might lose her before he could tell her how he felt about her. Beads of perspiration dribbled down his forehead and neck. The compression of people made it impossible for him to reach his handkerchief.

I'll find her, he told himself. I must. I will. Meanwhile, I'll create a plan to get her away from those ghouls, activate it step by step. Not slowly, for there isn't much time, yet do it with utmost care.

But I can do nothing until I find her. Sweat was gathering under his arms now. Chelsea, Chelsea, I can't lose you. Think, Yoshi, think!.

Reviewing the scene in Nara, he remembered Kagawa had abducted Chelsea immediately after learning about the afternoon appointment. Why? Because she might take the briefcase with her? If that were so, Kagawa could have taken them both back to Kyoto and kept the briefcase under his guard, allowing Chelsea to go wherever she wished. So, it also must be necessary to guard Chelsea. Her safety was important. She, too, must be guarded.

That was good, but why? Did it have something to do with that damned envelope hidden in that damned briefcase? He felt in the middle of a soap opera.

A few heads away, an attractive young woman looked up and smiled at him. Involuntarily, he smiled back. She giggled. A bespectacled man looked sternly at the woman. Once again she was lost among a sea of heads.

Yoshi glanced at his watch. A half hour until Kyoto. In the best scenario, Kagawa would take Chelsea back to the inn. If she was there, he would talk to her, tell her not to worry, that he didn't mind her not going to Grandmother's house. Then he would attend the tea ceremony alone. After that, plenty of time to figure out what to do: devise a strategy for ditching Kagawa and taking Chelsea to the airport himself.

And if she wasn't at the inn? What then?

Then he would interrogate the ladies who worked there to glean any possible information. Perhaps they would know where Kagawa might be; perhaps he told them where to send Chelsea's suitcase. Or they might have heard him talking on the phone.

If that didn't work, he would go to the police and file a missing-person report.

If all else failed, tomorrow, when she was supposed to fly back to the U.S. he would go to the airport at dawn, find out which Japan Airlines flight she was taking—surely he could ferret out that information, Then we would book a flight with her and wait until she arrived. No way would he lose Chelsea. No way!

****

Kagawa sat on a stool beside the entrance to Chelsea's room. He looked up from his magazine and glowered at Yoshi.

"Is Miss Jarvis in her room?" Yoshi inquired politely, attempting to keep his lips from trembling.

Kagawa rose from the stool. "Yes."

"I—I wish to speak with her."

"Sorry. Miss Jarvis has no more time for you. She is busy. Please respect her need for privacy." Kagawa sat down and returned to his reading.

Yoshi stepped forward.

"Go away," Kagawa growled without looking up. "Do not bother her."

Yoshi considered the possibility of rushing at the shoji screen, thrusting it open, and leaping inside before Kagawa could stop him, but given his experience at Grandmother's, he doubted his ability. Most likely all he would get for his bold effort would be a punch in the nose.

"*Arigato*," Yoshi said, wondering why he was thanking the thug. He bowed, not meaning that either.

Kagawa nodded and grunted like a displeased pig.

Returning to his room, Yoshi hurried out his garden shoji. Chelsea's shutters were drawn, her room closed off. He jammed his feet into his zori and clumped over to investigate. Locked. The damned shutters were padlocked. He knocked gently on the wood and listened. No answer. He knocked again, louder. Again, nothing.

He glanced about the garden. A group of ladies wearing the yukata of the inn, stood watching him from the pink rhododendrons. At the other end of the garden, an older couple sat on a bench near the maple trees. They, too, watched.

"Chelsea," he called. "It's Yoshi!"

Still no answer.

"Chelsea!" he yelled. "It's Yoshi."

A man wearing glasses came out of the room next to Chelsea's, his chin drawn back into his neck, his face concerned.

Not wanting to create a repeat scene of the Nara noodle stand, Yoshi bowed to everyone and clumped back to his room, where he noted with alarm that it was time to head for Grandmother's house.

No need to panic, he tried to assure himself. At least Chelsea was here at the inn, supposedly in her room. He would contact her this evening when it was dark and the garden deserted. He would beat on her shutters and hope the man in the next room sat close to his TV. If the man came out, he would sing and act drunk. He had heard that in Japan that was a more acceptable excuse for strange behavior.

But why were Chelsea's shutters padlocked? Was it to protect her from thieves? To keep her from going anyplace? Was she really busy? Was someone in the room with her? What was happening in there? Again his panic rose. Calm down, Yoshi told himself. It would never do for Grandmother to see me in this condition. He lifted his arms up and down to air out the sweat.

He threw off his suit, shirt and tie and pulled on his sweat pants and a T-shirt. Not until the foyer man with the polished head handed over his tennis shoes and white socks instead of his brown dress shoes and brown socks did Yoshi realize his outfit was all wrong. And he had left his room in shambles, clothes scattered about. What would the ladies of the inn think? And his Grandmother—she would feel insulted, her grandson appearing for tea in his running clothes. No time to go back to the room and change. He flailed his arms up and down some more.

The little shoe man flinched. He tossed Yoshi's tabi into the laundry bin and stepped back, his eyes wide.

"Excuse me," Yoshi said, hurriedly putting on his socks and shoes. "I do this when I sweat."

From the expression on the man's face, Yoshi realized he didn't understand English. *Atsui desu*, Yoshi said, to tell him he was hot. He charged out of the inn and threaded through the maze of streets toward Grandmother's house, his blood racing, his thoughts jumbled.

By the time he arrived at Grandmother's gate, the idea of kneeling through a long tea ceremony was more than he could bear. He would ask her to please forgive him. She would think him a clumsy oaf with no manners, but she probably thought that already. Now, appearing in such awful looking clothes made him seem even more unmannerly. How would he ever redeem himself?

He rang the little bell outside her entrance, then rushed through the gate. From inside he heard the shush-shush of her slippers moving across the tatami. The shoji opened. There she stood, dressed in an elegant gray kimono, her hands clasped over her chest. She bowed low and gestured for him to come inside.

"Grandmother," he cried, erupting into her room, forgetting about his shoes. "Terrible things have happened." He fell to his knees and in a mixture of Japanese and English spouted out the story about meeting Chelsea and going with her to Nara.

"She has this briefcase with a strange sealed envelope in it. Tomorrow she'll be forced to carry it on her plane to San Francisco. A man from the yakuza seized Chelsea from the noodle stand. I can't contact her because she's guarded in her room. She's in some sort of deep trouble, and I want to help her because I like her so much, but I'm such an oaf. I don't know what to do."

When he was done, Grandmother still had her hands clasped over her chest, but her eyes looked larger than normal. "Be still, Tsuyoshi," she said quietly. "The situation I understand."

"I must do something," he floundered. "There isn't much time. I have to help her."

She sighed. "*Hai, hai,* but first meet your Great Uncle Nagata." With dainty steps Grandmother shuffled toward the garden, the shoji already open. "Come, Tsuyoshi, come. Tea ceremony first." She looked back at him. "You need calm head. That best for difficult problems." She gestured to her garden. "Please, you follow."

CHAPTER 14

Chelsea woke up in darkness, feeling confused, her head throbbing. Where was she? With utmost concentration she gathered her splintered thoughts. Think, think, she told herself.

She realized she was lying on something soft, a warm cover over her. She was wearing only her bra and underpants. How odd! Why hadn't she put on her nightgown?

For a moment she thought she was a child in Los Angeles, recovering from the flu, her mother and father swilling whiskey in the other room as they often did.

But it was too quiet. No sound of their bickering. And she wasn't a child.

Her mind began to clear. Senses sharpened. She realized she was lying on a small mattress on the floor in the middle of a room that smelled of cedar. The object beside her was a lantern. She turned on the switch and a dim light illuminated the scene. Her hat rested on a low table by the wall. The mattress, a futon, a pair of tabi next to it. This was the Momiji-ya. She was in Kyoto. Somebody had undressed her.

She bolted into a sitting position. Who had undressed her? With a groan she sank back under the covers. Lord, how her head ached!

A bottle of aspirin might be in my suitcase, she thought. If I can pull myself together...make it to the closet...

She squinted at her watch—six o'clock, early evening, darker than it should be, outside shutters closed. Why now? Why did she feel this lousy? Again she looked at the low table. Then she remembered.

Oh, God, I drank the tea.

Chagrinned, she pulled the covers over her head. I allowed them to do this to me, she thought. They drugged me so I wouldn't go anyplace. Well, I won't let these guys trick me again. Do they really think that now I'll carry their damned letter to San Francisco? She threw back the covers. I'll show them.

She rose unsteadily and wavered to the closet. The inn's yukata was on a hanger. Next to it was her skirt, jacket, and blouse. They looked newly pressed, each piece hung separately. On the floor beside them her suitcase stood on end, her purse on top. But where was her briefcase. She dropped to her knees and searched all corners of the closet. She turned around and surveyed every part of the room. Gone. With it, her passport, plane ticket, laptop and the manila envelope.

Frantically, she searched through her purse and suit pockets. No cell phone either. Everything important, taken. All that was left in her purse was her makeup kit. The only items in her suit pockets were a packet of wipe-and-dries, the little dictionary and a tube of lipstick. She snapped open her suitcase. Fumbling around inside, she finally located the bottle of aspirin in a zippered pouch.

Thank God, I still have that, she thought, rising, holding onto the edge of the shoji for balance.

Clutching the bottle as if a thief might yank it away, she lurched toward the shoji that led to her bathroom.

What about Yoshi she wondered? Had he found his way back to the inn? Was he all right? In his room? She must talk to him. Make a plan. But first, recuperate, think more clearly.

At the sink, she threw cold water on her face and remembered Yoshi's appointment for the tea ceremony with his grandmother.

His honorable grandmother. She hoped he hadn't missed what was so important to him. She swallowed three aspirin and drank a full glass of water.

Her stomach growled.

Again she looked at her watch. Dinner should come soon. After that, she would feel better, think better. She had all night, until seven o'clock in the morning, departure time for the airport, to somehow retrieve her passport, plane tickets, cell phone and the damned envelope, find Yoshi, and escape to the countryside. Somehow, she would manage.

Gazing at herself in the mirror, she smiled wryly. Her looks weren't up to courtroom standard, her face the hue of a sliced cucumber and the dark crescents under her eyes a reflection of her eyebrows. She tried to brush back her bangs, but they stuck straight out like porcupine quills. With a groan of disgust, she threw more handfuls of cold water on her face and momentarily buried her head in a towel. I'll outwit these thugs, she told herself. I will, I will!

Retreating from the bathroom, she decided exercise might speed her recovery. She touched her toes three times, nearly falling over the last time. Then, remembering her first meeting with Yoshi, she executed a series of arm rolls. Feeling woozy, she sank down onto the futon. She felt weak and a little sick to her stomach. Best to eat dinner before trying any more exercises, she decided. She made it to her feet again and tiptoed to the hall shoji, sliding the screen back a few inches. There sat Kagawa on a stool, reading a magazine, her briefcase under his legs.

"*Ohayo gozaimas*," he growled.

"*Ohayo?*" she gasped. Is it really morning?

He nodded and continued reading.

Then she noted sunlight streaming in through the inn's foyer. She slid the screen shut with a bang and stumbled over to the garden shoji, thrust it open and tried to shove back the shutters. They wouldn't budge. Again she pushed. Locked from the outside. Daylight filtered through a crack—a tiny spear of light she hadn't noticed when she first woke up, her mind too fogged.

Her hands shook and her knees wobbled. Her tongue felt dry and bloated, the taste revolting. I'm weak because I've been drugged, she thought. No food. Not enough time for aspirin to work. Too much sleep.

Dizzy, she sank to her knees and crawled over to the futon. Holding the sides of her head, she tried hard to understand her situation. It's not six at night, she told herself. It's six in the morning. Morning, for God's sake. For fifteen hours I've been knocked out. Someone brought in the futon, took off my clothes and covered me up. Please, let it not have been Kagawa.

She shivered at that possibility.

In less than an hour, she thought, Kagawa will drive me to the airport. Or maybe to oblivion. Maybe he thinks I suspect too much. Plans to get rid of me. Think, Chelsea, think! Pull yourself together.

She heard a rap on the hall shoji frame.

"Yes?" she said, summoning authority to her voice.

"Miss Jarvis, I wish to speak with you?"

A male voice. Not Yoshi's, not Kagawa's but a voice that sounded familiar. "Just a minute," she called and staggered to the closet.

Figuring who most likely it was, she decided against the yukata and stepped into her skirt. The zipper caught on a seam. Hell! She took a deep breath and tried again. There. The blouse buttons gave her trouble. In disgust, she gave up on the bottom two and slipped on her jacket. Rushing into the bathroom, she leaned against the wall for a moment, and then reached into her pocket for her tube of lipstick. Blinking, trying her best to focus, she applied the gloss and blotted her lips on a piece of toilet paper. As she wavered toward the hall shoji, she managed the last two buttons and tucked in her blouse.

"Who is it?" she called, deciding not to open the shoji until she knew for sure.

"Mr. Hayashi."

Backing up, she smoothed the sides of her hair and tried to bring order to her bangs. She wished for her high heels. Towering over the guy might help. No, heels aren't necessary, she concluded. I'm taller than he is without them.

Her knees felt like jelly. It was all she could do to keep on her feet. She rubbed her still-throbbing temples, firmed her jaw and tried to stand straight.

"Come in," she called sharply. "I've been expecting you." A lie, but it might deal her a good card in a dubious hand.

He was even heavier than she remembered—as wide as tall, no neck, that ball of a head rising directly from his shoulders. Instead of the striped pants and tails, he wore a dark blue suit with a magenta shirt and flowered tie. His white gloves were still on. A red peony was clipped to his lapel.

He bowed low.

She nodded curtly.

He stepped into the room.

Behind him, the screen moved completely aside and the woman, who had so charmingly served the dinner in Yoshi's room, entered, breathing hard, lugging two, straight-backed, wooden chairs, the Western kind, one on either side of her diminutive body. Chelsea wanted to run over and help but sensed it would be a wrong move. Besides, probably right now she didn't have the strength.

Hayashi waved the woman to an area near the lantern, the only light in the room. She set the chairs down, facing each other, three feet apart, their frames casting long, bony shadows across the tatami. Intruders, Chelsea thought, grossly out of place in this traditional room.

The woman bustled about, folding up the futon, opening the pit, replacing the table and low chair, depositing the tabi beside Chelsea's chair. Once she gave Chelsea a sideways glance, no expression on her face, none of the bubbly humor of their last meeting. Chelsea kept track of her with peripheral vision, her main focus on Hayashi. He spoke in low tones to Kagawa, who stood in the screen opening. "*Hai, hai,*" Kagawa kept saying, his head bent over to his waist.

Hayashi smiled widely at Chelsea and indicated the chairs. Stiffly, she sat down. He waddled over and lowered himself with a grunt onto the other chair, hands resting on thighs, elbows elevated. Although he appeared to study the cedar-paneled ceiling, she knew he was observing her. She wished for more makeup and longed for her hat, still there on the table. Should she reach over and grab it? No, the move might be taken as a nervous gesture.

She noticed her closet door and suitcase still open. Did that make her appear in disarray? It's okay, she concluded. Hayashi's back is to the closet. She crossed her legs and arms, waiting, attempting to draw herself into full awareness.

A metal thump outside startled her. From the corner of her eye, Chelsea watched the great, wooden shutters open, clacking like the train that crossed the old wooden bridge in her childhood. The room filled with light, forcing her to blink several times.

The woman turned off the lantern and set it behind the TV. She snapped Chelsea's suitcase shut and set it on end in the closet. Picking Chelsea's hat up from the table, she dusted it off, and took it to the closet, setting it on top of her purse. For a moment the woman stood there, staring at Hayashi's back. She met Chelsea's eyes and with a quick motion reached into her obi, pulled out a piece of paper and tucked it under the hat. Quickly, she slid the closet screen shut. Shuffling forward, she knelt before Hayashi, her head deeply bowed, palms downward, fingers touching the tatami.

"*Mo yoroshii desuka,*" she said, wanting to know if there was anything else she could do. There was a slight quaver to her voice.

"*Ah ii,*" Hayashi replied, shaking his head. He waved her away.

The woman rose, backed off, and faded into the hallway, closing the shoji slowly, like a curtain drawn on a scene.

CHAPTER 15

"Did you enjoy your tour yesterday?" Mr. Hayashi asked.

"Up to a point," Chelsea replied.

He smiled and nodded. "I find Nara's gardens and temples quite restful. I go to the Kasuga Shrine when they light the stone lanterns. It is most beautiful then."

"I imagine so."

He continued smiling.

She realized he was scrutinizing her unruly bangs. I'm glad you find them amusing, she thought. Get too close and they'll stab you. She glared at his hands. At least my fingers don't look like boiled sausages.

"I must apologize," he said, shifting his eyes to his gloved hands. "In our society it is not polite to examine people. However, Miss Jarvis, I find you so fascinating I cannot help but look at you again and again."

"That doesn't bother me one bit."

He pursed his lips and raised his eyebrows as if her answer had surprised him.

The room grew so quiet she heard a cricket chirping among the maples across the garden. Finally, she asked, "Is there a particular reason why you came here to see me?"

His chair creaked as he shifted his heavy weight forward. "I thought you might wish to discuss recent events."

"Such as?"

He shrugged. "Have you no questions, Miss Jarvis? Please be frank with me."

"Of course I have questions." She spoke as pleasantly as possible. "Is it normal procedure in Japan for drivers to kidnap their passengers?"

His eyes widened. "Certainly not."

"Perhaps you can tell me if kidnapping is a common occurrence within your corporation?"

He stiffened. "It is not common."

"Then, why did your so-called 'guide' drag me away from my friend, shove me into his car, and race away from Nara, paying no attention to my protests and leaving my friend behind without transportation?"

"Your guide was protecting you from harm."

"So that's your rationalization. What's the excuse for dosing me with a knock-out drug?"

He bent his head to one side. "A knock-out drug?"

"You know what I mean. Was that also for my protection? Knocking me out for fifteen hours? No chance for dinner, no opportunity to stroll through the garden or sink into the reputedly relaxing bath in the wooden tub. Is this your usual treatment of guests?"

His hands flew out. "I had no idea you suffered such indignities. Someone must have tampered with your tea." He stood like a puppet jerked on a string. "I shall speak to management."

Chelsea wet her lips. "How did you know the drug was administered in my tea?"

He sat down and looked at the table as if the tea might still be there. "How else would a drug be administered? You said you had no dinner."

"It could have been placed in another drink."

"No, no. Our tradition is to have tea waiting in the room. It must have been in the tea."

"You know the drug was given to me in my room?"

He frowned. "I confess it was an assumption."

She raised her chin. "In my profession, Mr. Hayashi, nothing is assumed." She felt better, her headache dissipating, her mind clear and focused.

His wide smile reappeared. He returned his hands to his thighs. "Miss Jarvis, you must be quite a success in your profession."

"I manage fairly well." She matched his smile; it seemed the proper mask to wear.

"Perhaps now you are ready to question me more," he said, sounding slightly sarcastic.

"Yes, I'll admit I'm curious about a few other things."

"I shall be happy to enlighten you."

She glared at him. "Good. For starters, who undressed me?"

"A friend of mine."

"That ghoul Kagawa?"

A faint smile crossed his face. "No, the mistress of the inn. She thought you would be more comfortable with your suit off."

"So, the owner of the inn came in here, saw me passed out and her only concern was that I would be more comfortable without my suit?"

"I'm sure that was not her only concern. She immediately contacted me."

"Does she have my cell phone, laptop, passport, plane tickets..." She met his eyes. "And of course the sealed envelope—everything important?"

Hayashi shook his head. "Kagawa took them for safekeeping."

She leaned forward. "I'd like them back now."

"Sorry. That is not possible. We will return your cell phone and laptop after you complete customs in San Francisco. The other items will be returned to you at the Tokyo/Narita Airport."

"I'm an American citizen," she cried. "Do you really think you can do this?"

Abruptly he waved an arm. "Yes! I can do more than you realize." The tone of his voice was deadly. "You will say nothing about this to anybody."

Pressing her lips together, she considered threatening to contact authorities and expose him. She thought about standing up, making a big scene, screaming for help. But what if the inn was controlled by the yakuza? Threats were not the way for her to go, she concluded. Let him think he had her buffaloed. Find out why Hayashi was doing this.

Once again he gazed at the ceiling.

Silence filled the room.

At last she said, "May I continue with my questions, Mr. Hayashi?"

"Of course," he replied, meeting her eyes. His chair squeaked as he readjusted his heavy form.

She attempted a pleasant look. "I made an engagement to attend a tea ceremony with my friend, Tsuyoshi Moore. Why did Mr. Kagawa prevent me from going there with him?"

"Ah, your friend, Mr. Moore. He is a dangerous man."

"In what way?"

"He plans to steal the envelope I entrusted to you."

Chelsea crossed her arms and frowned. "What makes you think Mr. Moore is a thief?"

"It is more than an assumption." His smile returned." I have strong reasons to believe it so."

She waited for the reasons, but he gave none. "Why would he want your envelope?" she continued.

The smile left Hayashi's face. "For what is inside."

"Which is?"

For a moment he said nothing. Then he answered, speaking slowly, seeming to consider his choice of each word. "A valuable document. It is worth a vast amount of money."

Chelsea straightened her back. Swallowing hard, she said, "Why don't you send the document electronically? Isn't that how business is usually done these days?"

As though his seat had grown uncomfortable, he shifted his weight. "Yes, but it was not wise to send this document electronically." His voice hardened. "Miss Jarvis, my business is complex. I have no time to spend delving into its intricacies."

"Look, Mr. Hayashi, I'm a licensed California attorney, not a common letter carrier. I deserve a hell of a lot more explanation before I'll carry an envelope whose contents aren't known to me."

A hint of anger touched his face, then left. He rolled his eyes and heaved a sigh. "Other companies continually tap my networks. Mr. Hunter told me you and he were"—he shrugged—

"close friends. Since you were here, there seemed no reason why you would not wish to carry my valuable envelope to him, one I did not trust sending by any type of mail." He paused. "An envelope whose contents I do not wish to broadcast to my rivals."

"So, you conned me into traipsing out of Japan with an extremely valuable document in my briefcase."

"Traipsing?"

"Yes, traipsing. Why didn't you tell me this before?"

"I did not believe my business was your concern." He sneered. "Besides, you did not ask me."

She glowered at him. "By chance, did Mr. Hunter inform you not to worry, that I was an ethical attorney who would not pry into sealed correspondence?"

"Yes, he did tell me that."

"Hm-m-m." She brushed an imaginary speck from her skirt. "Why are you sending this document to Mr. Hunter?"

"To invest for our corporation."

"I see. Well, no, I don't, but I'm beginning to understand."

He wrinkled his nose as if her understanding wasn't important to either of them.

She considered the possibilities. Eric couldn't bring the envelope through customs because he knew authorities suspected him of smuggling. For years he may have found ways to launder yakuza money in the US, depositing it in secret bank accounts or investing it in businesses, legal or illegal, his travel office a front for underhanded dealings. By setting up his business, she may have unwittingly assisted in unlawful activities.

And Yoshi? The thought of him as a dangerous thief seemed ridiculous. But could his shyness, the story about his Grandmother, his professorship of English—could all of that be a lie, a story to gain her confidence? She closed her eyes, praying Yoshi was not involved in deception, that somehow he would help her escape from these crooks. What if his plan was to help her escape, then steal the envelope and desert her?

Hayashi cleared his throat.

She looked around. "Oh, I'm sorry. I was considering my precarious predicament here."

He frowned. "I had nothing to do with your tea being drugged."

"I didn't accuse you. I asked questions."

"True, but I must assure you I am innocent of that regrettable situation."

"In our country, Mr. Hayashi, much of what you do would be more than regrettable. It would be criminal."

He shrugged. "I shall find out who drugged you and make certain the guilty culprit is punished." He rose. "You must be hungry. I do not wish to hold up your breakfast." He extended his arms magnanimously. "Since there is nothing more I can do for you here, I shall go. Mr. Kagawa will give you further instructions. I trust you will have a safe flight home." He bowed and started for the hall.

"Mr. Hayashi—"

He turned back.

"What if I refuse to take your envelope to Mr. Hunter?"

"You *shall* deliver it," he replied, his words spoken slowly and with force. "There will be no problem. Mr. Kagawa will be on the plane for your protection."

She drew in a quick breath.

Hayashi continued, "He will sit in the seat directly across the aisle and guard you and your briefcase all the way to San Francisco."

"Then let him carry the envelope," she snapped.

Hayashi's eyes turned to slits. His voice grew deep and ominous. "You will carry my envelope through customs and deliver it to my agent, Mr. Eric Hunter. Furthermore, as Mr. Kagawa will instruct, you must not speak to anyone about this matter. There are those who would go to any extreme to steal this envelope." He paused. "Be careful. Your life depends upon your actions. I have ways of making certain my orders are followed. Let me add that my network is wide and my people most efficient. *Sayonara*, Miss Jarvis." He inclined his head slightly and left, closing the screen behind him.

For a moment she couldn't move, stunned by his words. Then, she tiptoed to the hall shoji, opened it a crack, and peered out.

Kagawa sat on the stool reading a magazine, her briefcase tucked under his legs.

Hayashi must be the leader of the yakuza syndicate, she decided, or at least an important figure, for Kagawa followed his orders as if he were the Prince of Darkness. She inched the screen closed as if a sharp move might cause an explosion.

Something about the document in the envelope must be illegal, she thought. Stolen perhaps, something custom's officials were searching for. And, she concluded, Hayashi believed the safest way to get it to Eric was via a Caucasian American woman, an attorney who would normally carry a briefcase full of papers in which a manila envelope could be buried, carried by an honest-looking, one-time visitor to Japan, someone that customs officials would not suspect.

Deciding to run to Yoshi's room by way of the garden, she hurried over and slid that shoji open.

A guttural voice outside snarled, "Do not come out."

It was the thick-lipped man in dark glasses. He shoved her back into the room and pulled the shoji shut.

She tried to reopen the screen. It wouldn't move. He must be out there holding it. "Shit!" Gingerly she rubbed her arm that bore the man's finger marks.

It was then that she remembered the paper the little woman had hidden under her hat. As if someone might be watching, she edged open the closet shoji, snatched the paper out from under her hat and rushed to the bathroom, seemingly the safest place to take it. Once there, she opened the folded piece of paper.

If you need help,
when you leave your room
carry your hat in your left hand.
Yoshi

Wadding up the paper, she tossed it into the toilet, flushed it down and returned to her room. A lump built in her throat. She wanted to believe he cared about her safety. So much wanted to believe. But, if he was only after the document, by God, she would find a way to fight him as well.

CHAPTER 16

It was Kagawa who served her breakfast: soup, rice, broiled fish, tsukemono, and tea. Elbows angled out, arms held chest high, he carried the tray in the same manner he had carried her briefcase. With a grunt, he stooped over and set the tray on her table.

"We leave in twenty minutes," he announced and stared at the tray as if waiting for her response.

She looked away from him and made no reply.

"I come back to pick up your suitcase," he continued.

From the corner of her eye she watched him glance around as if making sure he had forgotten nothing. Damned robot, she thought. He pulled back his shoulders and left the room.

Her stomach churned. How could she eat breakfast? Yet she knew the importance of regaining stamina, needing fuel for energy. She felt weak, a little dizzy. Except for aspirin and water, nothing had entered her stomach since the drugged tea, no food since the Nara noodles. Unfortunately, the two packets of Alka-Seltzer she desperately needed were in her briefcase.

Then she remembered the antacid tablets.

Yes. She jumped up and nearly fell over, reaching down to the table to balance herself. Antacid tablets are in my make-up kit, she remembered. In my purse.

Staggering to the closet, she retrieved the package as if it were gold, and chomped up five tablets. Her jaws hurt. Her teeth felt gritty, on edge.

Okay, Jarvis. Now, go back and eat, she commanded herself.

The food tasted surprisingly good, especially the rice. She ate everything but the pickles. At first she viewed the pot of tea with distrust. Then she decided they wouldn't dare drug her now, not if they wanted her to walk onto the plane in a normal manner. She drank the contents of the pot and felt better, her headache nearly gone, stomach relaxing. If only she could sit here all morning in this peaceful room, the garden at her fingertips, sunlight filtering through the shoji. A glance at her watch brought her up tight. Only five minutes left.

In the bathroom she brushed her teeth vigorously and spent two intensive minutes on her makeup. Off to the closet, where she carefully picked up the bowler in her left hand. She stowed her toothbrush and toothpaste into her suitcase, snapping it shut with determination. Her makeup kit went into her purse. She pulled up the handle on her roller suitcase and stood in front of the hall shoji. A series of deep-breathing exercises concluded her preparations. One minute to spare.

Stay calm, she told herself. Whatever happens, don't lose your cool.

But her mind was so jumbled with questions that she felt a trickle of sweat down her back and her hands turned icy. Was Yoshi in his room? Peering at the hallway? Hiding outside the inn? Would he see her at all? Had he disappeared? Given up on her? Decided she wasn't worth the trouble? Was the thick-lipped man guarding him?

Even if Yoshi were free and wanted to help, what could he do? How could he overpower Kagawa? And what if Yoshi planned to grab the sealed envelope for his own gain? Was he as dangerous as the yakuza?

Or, what if the contents of the envelope were stolen and officials were searching for them? If discovered on her, she would be the guilty party. Off to prison. End of career. If she gave the envelope to the Japanese police, would they believe that she, an attorney whose purpose in Tokyo was to negotiate a contract with Hayashi, was not a willing participant in his other operations? If she carried the envelope through customs but failed to deliver it to Eric, would she get shot or even worse treated to a tortuous, slow death.

She clutched her suitcase handle to steady herself. Her shoulders slumped, depression overwhelming her.

Am I forced to do what these bastards want—be a part of their smuggling operation? If it weren't so, Eric or Kagawa would take the envelope through customs. They need someone who, most likely won't be searched. Me! Damn you, Eric, for getting me involved.

The thought of that deceitful toad with his smiling face and fanciful ways infuriated her. To think that for a year she had not once suspected her lover, her fun companion, her relaxation after a day in the grueling office. She had been happy to help him set up his travel corporation, had looked forward to seeing him every day after work. Would authorities believe she knew nothing about the yakuza, which probably ran his business? As Eric's girlfriend, she could right now be under suspicion. From the moment she took the envelope, she might be bait for someone's trap.

Calm down, Jarvis, calm down, she told herself and straightened her back.

Kagawa entered her room on time. He wore his usual white gloves, a corporate tradition she supposed, certainly a way to hide the fact he had no little fingers.

"We go now!" he commanded, grasping the handle of her suitcase. "Where is your purse?"

She returned to the closet and threw the purse strap across her right shoulder. "I wasn't going to forget it," she snapped, banging the closet shoji closed. She stood at attention. "There! Satisfied!"

He grunted approval. "Why don't you wear your hat?"

"I prefer to carry it. I'm hot. My head's on fire."

He snickered.

"Happy to amuse you."

In the hall, the thick-lipped man waited with her briefcase and another bag. At least he wasn't guarding Yoshi, she thought, relieved. She stalked past him, aware he fell in behind her, Kagawa ahead, elbows angled out. Down the tatami halls in single file they padded on slippered feet. She didn't dare look at any side shoji, in case Yoshi stood behind one, peering out through a crack. Somehow her body language might give away his presence. She kept her eyes forward, matching her leader's steps, her hat held in her left hand.

In the foyer, three sets of shoes awaited in a neat row below the bench, Chelsea's high heels in the middle. She sat down, sandwiched between Kagawa and the thick-lipped man, her body squeezed up, not wanting to touch either of them. She took off her slippers and jammed her feet into her shoes.

The shoe-keeper picked up the three pair of discarded slippers and placed them in a basket. He withdrew to the corner, where the top of his bowed, bald head glowed in the sunlight.

The thought of her slippers, still warm from her feet, commingled with those of the yakuza, disgusted Chelsea. It was like throwing their underwear together. She gave an involuntary shudder and then, with as much dignity as she could muster, emerged from the inn, still clutching her hat in her left hand.

The morning air was warm and jasmine-scented, the narrow street lined with small, unpainted wooden houses, meticulously kept. Trees, bright green with new leaves, splashed color against the pale sky. No sign of Yoshi; what could he do anyway? The Cadillac limousine, the hearse-like vehicle, waited at the curb. Involuntarily, she shivered. Was it carrying her to her grave?

Get your mind off the morbid track, she told herself. It invited disaster. Focus on planned strategy. That was the way to win.

Kagawa ushered her into the back seat of the limousine. She noted the thick-lipped man stowed her suitcase and the other piece of luggage, must be Kagawa's, in the car trunk. Kagawa set his briefcase on the floorboard of the front seat. A flurry of bows—Kagawa and the thick-lipped man to the mistress of the inn, she back to them. The two men climbed into the front seat, the thick-lipped man the driver. The locks clicked. The limousine glided forward, moving so smoothly it seemed she flew on a magic carpet.

The air conditioner swished on. Music wafted out—Gershwin's "Manhattan Suite." Here I am, she mused, locked in a Detroit-made car, driven by gangsters in American-style suits, listening to music about New York. How ironic!

At the train station, Kagawa removed the two pieces of luggage from the trunk. Setting his bag on top of her wheeled-suitcase he pulled the two along with his left hand and carried the briefcase in the other. "Stay beside me," he growled. "We go to through gates to the Bullet Train platform."

The thick-lipped man drove the limousine away.

Good, she thought as she walked with Kagawa. Henceforth, one on one. No sign of Yoshi though. Halfway to the train, she momentarily considered dashing off, hiding in the crowd. No, impossible without her briefcase. She would be left destitute. Besides, she was too tall to assimilate.

On the Bullet Train they sat side by side in the more expensive Green Section. A uniformed lady distributed hot, damp towels to the passengers. Chelsea considered mouthing "help" but couldn't remember the Japanese word for it. She pulled out her pocket dictionary. Kagawa reached over and snatched it away, inserting the little book into her suitcase. The uniformed lady left the car.

Chelsea noticed that all of the passengers on the train were Japanese. Did any of them speak English? They all looked engrossed in something—the men reading newspapers or working on computers; the women mostly looking at the scenery.

Abruptly she stood up, still holding her hat.

"What are you doing?" rasped Kagawa.

"Going to the bathroom," she said, slipping past him and heading for the rest room she remembered passing as they entered the train.

Kagawa followed her. As she entered, he grabbed her arm and said, "If you lock the door, I have a tool to unlock it from the outside."

She jerked her arm away and went inside, slamming the door behind her.

After relieving herself, she washed her hands and stared a moment at her unruly bangs. Why not make Kagawa come in and drag her out, create a scene. She sighed and dismissed the idea, envisioning Kagawa saying she was a crazy tourist, frightened about Japan, and he had been entrusted to take her to the airport. Or another yakuza on the train arriving to help him. Or nobody on the train wanting to be involved. Wasn't that a Japanese trait? Anyway, without her airline tickets, passport and money what could she do? He even had her dictionary. She opened the door, glared at Kagawa and returned to her seat.

As the train shot past cities interspersed with rice fields, Mt. Fuji glowing behind like a painted backdrop, Chelsea sat stiffly, formulating a plan. After they reached the Narita Airport, as they walked toward Security, she would insist on carrying her briefcase, telling Kagawa that it would raise suspicion to transfer it at the last minute. Along the way, near a woman's rest room, she would pretend to turn her ankle, shriek, and impose on bystanders to help her to a seat. Hopefully this would draw a crowd. At a strategic moment, she would ask a young, intelligent-looking woman to assist her into the rest room, taking the briefcase with her. If Kagawa tried to retrieve it, she would scream that the contents could not be trusted to that terrible stranger. Once inside the rest room, she would ask the woman to slip out and locate police, explain that the man out there had molested her and should be arrested. She would caution the woman to stay clear of Kagawa. When the police arrived, Chelsea would tell her story, hand over the envelope and beg for protection.

But what if no crowd gathered at the terminal? Or if the crowd consisted only of men? Or if the woman she chose spoke no English? The Japanese police might never show up. Kagawa might have no qualms about charging into a ladies' rest room to drag her out. If the police did arrive, Kagawa might bribe them or convince them she had stolen an envelope from him or pull yakuza strings. She might be arrested instead. Even if the plan worked out, what about protection after she returned to San Francisco?

Too many chances for that plan to go wrong, she decided.

She closed her eyes and wondered if it would be better to solve these problems in America rather than in a foreign country, what with the language problem and her high visibility here. If Yoshi were with her, she might evaporate into the countryside, but by herself, little chance of doing it without quick apprehension. Surely, during the plane ride she would find an opportunity to speak to a flight attendant and explain her problem. Maybe then....

Her eyes flew open. Why hadn't Eric booked her return flight through Osaka? That was an airport closer to Kyoto? Did the yakuza need a particular flight? Certain officials? Certain plane crew?

Two hours later the Bullet Train reached Tokyo. Kagawa at her elbow, Chelsea joined a river of people, flowing up the stairs to the exit. At the curb was the white limousine with little Mr. Tamiyasu, motionless as a mannequin, standing on his stool, crimson flower protruding from his buttonhole. Directly ahead was the Emperor's Palace surrounded by a host of perfectly pruned pine trees and a number of police boxes. No sign of Yoshi. Once more she thought of shouting for help. Of running for the police boxes. Would they help her or recognize the yakuza connection and stay away?

As if he read her thoughts, Kagawa dropped the suitcases and pushed her into the back seat of the limousine and shut the door. The rear door locks clicked. Kagawa climbed into the front passenger seat with the briefcase while Mr. Tamiyasu stowed their baggage in the trunk.

The drive to Narita Airport was slow—roads traffic-clogged. She didn't like the music, Prokofiev. She tried to dismiss the memory of it, tried not to listen. Her mother used to play a CD of this piece, driving her father from the house with its volume. She stared through the window at the line of cars on the expressway, a mass of parallel lives unable or too busy to reach each other.

I'll carry the envelope to America, she concluded. Once in San Francisco, I'll call up the FBI and request their protection. I'll disappear. My law partners will help me. I'll hide in that home for orphaned children that Jan and Logan founded. Or I'll escape to the Warners' ski cabin on Donner Summit. Surely McCloskey or Warner can cover my cases until the yakuza gang focuses on other problems.

She frowned. But how can I leave my clients and associates in the lurch? And what about the Thomson trial? Anyway Hayashi and Kagawa would never forget me.

The limousine pulled up to the terminal entrance. The locks clicked. Mr. Tamiyasu opened her door and bowed low. Airport noise blasted.

CHAPTER 17

The crowd was dense and loud, the air stifling, smelling of jet fuel. Intent on his duties, Mr. Tamiyasu scurried to the trunk to retrieve the suitcases.

A uniformed man appeared—short, gray-haired, officious. He insisted on checking their baggage. Kagawa seemed annoyed at the intrusion, but showed him the two boarding passes, probably not wanting to cause a commotion. The man attached tags, gave stubs to Kagawa, and then evaporated into the crowd, a bag under each arm.

Chelsea looked around. Still no sign of Yoshi. Kagawa leaned in close to her. She jerked away, his breath reminding her of steam from a sewer vent. Then, realizing he wanted to tell her something, she allowed him to speak into her ear.

"Walk into the terminal and head for security," Kagawa hissed. "I will be close behind you."

After they passed through the doorway, he indicated the line ahead, divided by loosely roped stanchions. He whispered, "When we near the line, I give you your briefcase, boarding pass and passport." He glanced around. "In the line, I stay two persons behind you all the way. After your documents are checked, head for the far right scanning station. I go through the one next to it. Most likely they search me more than you. After you pass through security, sit on the right hand bench and wait for me. Go no further until I arrive. You will be watched and guarded. Do you understand?"

She nodded, realizing the scanner in the far right station must be run by Hayashi's people. What would happen, she thought, if I went to another station? *You will be watched and guarded,* Kagawa had said. Should I try it?

As they neared the line, Kagawa handed over her passport, boarding pass and briefcase.

In her profession Chelsea had used her case not only for transporting files and pushing through crowds but as an office and courtroom prop—dropped dramatically, shoved across her desk, kicked away, slammed on a table. Maybe she could use it here in some wild fashion. Think, Chelsea, think.

It was not as hot in the rope-divided line that slowly snaked forward. Chelsea noticed the coolness came from a large, high fan that blew air over the people. She glanced back. Two people stood between her and Kagawa. The line seemed to take forever.

Half way through, she made a decision. I'm not going to the right-hand scanning station. I'll take the next one over. Bang down my case. Scream for help. It's worth a try.

She was close to the document-checking officer when an old woman in a kimono, apparently confused, backed under the rope from another section of the line, a large fiber bag in her arms. With profuse apologies to Kagawa, the woman insisted, using multiple gestures, that she didn't know what had happened. She appeared to have difficulty balancing her bag. With little chirps, she readjusted its load.

Unexpectedly, the old woman squealed. Somehow, the contents of her fiber bag tumbled out. A flood of rice crackers and chestnuts clacked down around Kagawa's feet. The befuddled woman threw up her hands and the last item in her bag, a bottle of sake, crashed to the floor, breaking into a thousand pieces, spraying Kagawa's highly polished shoes.

"*Sumimasen, sumimasen,*" the poor woman lamented, falling to her knees and wiping Kagawa's shoes with a silk cloth produced from her kimono sleeve.

Kagawa tried to push the lady away. A security officer came up and a heated conversation ensued.

Someone touched Chelsea's shoulder. She turned. Yoshi!

He indicated the nearest terminal exit. Snatching her hat, he grabbed her left hand and pulled her along, ducking under separation ropes until they were free of the line. Before going out the door, Chelsea looked back. In front of Kagawa stood a man in uniform, shouting orders into a radio phone. The old woman and a few other people in the line were crawling around, retrieving crackers, chestnuts and bits of broken glass.

Outside, Yoshi deftly led her through the crowd toward the curb. A small, white car waited, rear door open, motor running. She fell into the back seat. Yoshi slipped in after her, yanked the door shut and then locked it.

"Stay down," he commanded.

She crouched, her briefcase on the floor beside her feet.

The car edged into the stream of traffic. For a long time she kept her head lowered.

Finally the driver said, "Okay. Nobody follow. Good job, folks."

Chelsea rose up. The driver shot a welcoming smile over his shoulder. To her amazement, it was the man who had checked the baggage.

Yoshi said, "Meet Great Uncle Nagata. Great Uncle Nagata, this is my friend Chelsea Jarvis."

"*Ohayo, gozaimas*" the uncle shouted without looking back.

"*Ohayo*," she managed to reply.

Tears filled her eyes and spilled onto her cheeks. She had no idea why. She wasn't sad. Not hurt. Never had cried in public.

She faced her window, not wanting Yoshi to see her cry, although she didn't want people outside to see her either. What does it matter, she told herself. Gaining some control, she said to Yoshi, "I'd about decided you wouldn't show up."

"I had to help you."

"Didn't see how you could. Those damn thugs are so organized." She fumbled in her jacket pocket for a tissue, then blew her nose and, looking away, wiped her eyes.

After a bit, she felt recovered enough to begin the interrogation and establish her position. With a calculating look at Yoshi, she retrieved her hat and jammed it back on her head. "I doubt if it's me you care to save," she said, trying to keep her voice steady.

He looked perplexed.

"You want the manila envelope, don't you?"

"Why should I want that?"

"It's worth lots of money."

Yoshi's eyes bulged. "Why? What's in it?"

"Don't know."

Great Uncle Nagata peered over his shoulder, a worried look on his face.

Yoshi said, "Chelsea, I'm not after that envelope." He put an arm around her, drew her close.

She didn't resist, too tired and drained to pull away. Besides, his arm was warm, and she wanted it around her no matter what his motives were.

"Do you really think that's why I helped you?" he asked. "For the contents of that envelope?" He tilted her face up, searching her eyes. "Not everyone wants something from you or is trying to defeat you."

How honest he looks, she thought. How believable he sounds. Yet the old inner voice told her to hold a reserve, to keep a distance. Each time she had believed in a man, the hurt had cut deeper.

She said, "In my personal life I've occasionally trusted the wrong people. As a result..." Aware her words sounded stilted, she stopped but then plunged on anyway. "It's made me pretty cautious about my relationships."

"I understand, but I have no intention of pushing our relationship. And I have no ulterior motives. I wanted to help you because—" He swallowed. "Because I like what I know of you." "And," he added shyly, "I'd like to know you better."

Chelsea drew a deep breath and blew it out forcibly. "Okay, Yoshi, okay, I'll take a chance on you, because...well, because I'd like to know you better, too." She squeezed his arm.

"Good deal!" cried Great Uncle Nagata. *"Daijobu, daijobu.* Now everybody pay attention to road. No tell who comes racing after us." He braked the car so a young woman with a child bundled on her back could cross the street.

Chelsea leaned on Yoshi's shoulder. I have to believe in someone, she thought. After a few moments of silence, she looked up at him. "I wonder who that old lady was? The little woman who spilled her basket?"

"My grandmother," Yoshi replied.

"Good Lord!"

He nodded. "Yes, she continues to surprise me. I didn't expect her to be so brave and clever."

"What about her safety? Kagawa might drag her off—even kill her."

The uncle said over his shoulder, "My sister too old for that. Not Japanese way with elderly to interfere. Bad manners." His free arm shot out, karate chopping the air.

"But when Kagawa notices I'm gone," Chelsea continued, "he might forget his manners. These guys don't seem too nice."

Again the hand slice. "If so, Toru handle."

Yoshi explained, "Toru is Great Uncle Nagata's son. He's going to college right now, but he used to work at the airport as a security officer. So, he dusted off his uniform and appeared at the strategic moment. If all went according to Grandmother's plan, then Toru's calling for a clean-up crew was another distraction so he could escort wailing Grandmother away, blood dripping from a cut in her hand."

"Blood?" Chelsea's eyes widened. "She planned to cut herself?"

"No, no," Yoshi cried. " She had a packet of catsup hidden in her obi."

Chelsea laughed. "I'd love to meet your grandmother."

"You shall. She's coming to Great Uncle Nagata's house. That's where we're headed. All of us will spend the night there. That is, if Grandmother's plan is completely successful."

Great Uncle Nagata cried, "No worry, Tsuyoshi. Toru fix." His hand whipped about. "He black-belt. I taught."

"I'm impressed," Chelsea said. "Yoshi, how did you manage to convince your family to help me?"

"I told Grandmother and Great Uncle Nagata the problem. They took it from there. I'll admit I was amazed. In Japan, it's unusual for anyone to interfere with yakuza plans."

"*Hai*" the uncle agreed. "Scary people, but crisis time for family. Matter of pride and necessity."

"Commendable," she murmured, remembering how different it had been when a crisis occurred in her own family.

They were entering the town of Odawara, its massive feudal castle cresting the central hill. Great Uncle Nagata kept to the side streets. Then, he turned the car into a narrow empty lane, drove slowly part way down and stopped. "This is it," he said softly.

Yoshi could only open the door part way because of a fence. He squeezed outside and studied the scene ahead and behind. "Nobody in sight,' he whispered in to Chelsea.

"My house is through that gate." the uncle said quietly, nodding his head toward it.

Chelsea picked up her briefcase and said to him, "*Do mo arigato.*"

"*Do itashimashite,*" he replied. "*Dozo, odaiji ni.*"

Although she didn't understand the last part, the words sounded reassuring. She slipped outside and gently closed the door.

While Yoshi retrieved her bag from the trunk, she pressed her back against the car, feeling vulnerable, thinking she created a target but not daring to move ahead. Her eyes darted about in frantic assessment of two other gates that opened onto the lane. Kagawa could hide behind any one. Temporary jitters, she concluded. Unique situation. Even in court she often waited to find out what must be countered before she made her move.

Great Uncle Nagata lowered his window and whispered, "No worry. All okay."

Yoshi squeezed past her, suitcase held high. "Thanks for your help, Great Uncle. *Ja, atode.*" Respectfully, he lowered his head.

"*Hai, mata.*" The gray-haired man touched the window sill with his forehead. "I must get back to my job at the airport. This evening I come back home."

Yoshi nodded. After a quick look about, he sprinted a few steps beyond the car. On the right, he lifted the latch of a tall wooden gate. Attached to its center was a small bronze tiger, jaws open, eyes fierce.

CHAPTER 18

As the car drove away, Chelsea hurried through the gate, glad to see Yoshi come in behind her and close it. From someplace she heard a bell tinkling.

They stood in a stone, plant-lined courtyard no bigger than the foyer at the Momiji-ya. Ahead was an unpainted, wooden building, topped by a roof of vivid blue tiles, their shiny surfaces looking wet in the angled sunlight.

A young woman emerged from the doorway. Over her blouse and slacks she wore a smock-like apron, on her head, a scarf tied in back beneath long, black hair. Smiling and bowing, she took Chelsea's suitcase and gestured for them to enter the house. *Dozo oide kudasai,* she murmured. Chelsea gathered they were words of welcome.

After they were inside, Yoshi explained to Chelsea that this was Toru's wife and that she and Toru lived here with Great Uncle Nagata, Toru's father.

The front room looked about eight by twelve feet; the only other room—the bedroom, she assumed—looked even smaller. Chelsea didn't see how three people could live together in such a small house. Were she and Yoshi also going to sleep in this house overnight? If so, there would be five people, and if Yoshi's grandmother joined them, six. Where would they all sleep?

The furnishings were western-style: gray couch and coffee table opposite the front door and a TV and stereo system that matched the pearl gray walls, a shade lighter than the tiled floor. Next to the L-shaped kitchen was a glossy white dining table with three matching chairs. The only colors in the room came from a large red and yellow Picasso print hung above the couch and a multi-colored Shinto altar on a corner shelf. No shojis in sight. Everything looked neat to the point of perfection, as if a speck of dust might tip an alarm.

The young woman closed the front door. In a high-pitched voice she conversed in Japanese with Yoshi, and then, after a modest smile at Chelsea, carried the suitcase into the other room. Chelsea glimpsed a western-style double-sized bed. Had sleeping arrangements been determined? Yoshi's suitcase must be in there too.

"Tonight you'll sleep in the other room," Yoshi said as if he read her mind.

"All of us?"

"No. Just you."

"I don't want to take over their bedroom."

"It would be an insult to refuse their hospitality."

"Where will they sleep?"

"Out here."

"Along with your grandmother and Great Uncle Nagata?"

He nodded.

"You too?"

"Sure. Enough space, enough futons. Great Uncle Nagata sleeps this way all the time."

Chelsea wasn't sure if it was the traditional way of treating an honored guest or the cool breath of cultural isolation. Never had she experienced this sort of situation—a family flocking to her aid, sharing their home with her, bunking in the living room for her benefit. Although she appreciated it, she felt uneasy, different, embarrassed.

The young woman returned. Eyes lowered, she spoke to Chelsea in heavily accented but carefully proper English, her voice not quite as high as before. "Welcome to our home, Miss Jarvis. My name is Kayoko. I am wife to Toru."

"Nice to meet you, Kayoko. Just call me Chelsea."

"Chel-sea." She cocked her head to one side and blinked. "Very pretty name." She giggled. Covering her mouth and hunching her shoulders, she said, "Excuse me, Chel-sea. I tea for you fix. Please, you sit. Be comfort—ah, what is the word—comforty?"

"Comfortable?" Chelsea suggested.

"M-m-m, yes. Be comfortable." She scurried to the stove.

Fifteen minutes later, while they drank tea, the gate bell tinkled again.

Kayako and Yoshi exchanged anxious looks. "Stay here," Yoshi said to Chelsea. "If it's someone searching for you, I'll find a way to get rid of him. Go in the other room. If necessary, hide under the bed. He set down his teacup and hurried out into the courtyard. Kayako followed, closing the front door behind her. Chelsea stood, listening, nervous, ready to flee. The third cup was a dead give away. Three people here. She rushed to the sink with her cup.

Then she heard Yoshi cry, "Grandmother! Toru! Great Uncle Nagata!" Tentatively, she opened the front door a crack, relieved to see the three coming into the courtyard.

There stood Grandmother, so little and fragile a puff of wind might blow her over. Chelsea found it hard to believe that this delicate woman, who now patted Yoshi's arms as if fluffing up a pillow, had outwitted a yakuza thug. No sign of blood on her now; she wore a fresh kimono. Next to Grandmother stood the young airport official, Toru, a package under one arm, his uniform jacket looped over the other, his head bobbing up and down like a tightly wound, mechanical toy. And there was Great Uncle Nagata. They all faced each other in the small courtyard, bowing and talking in Japanese. Should she go out and join in the family greeting? Or not? Hard to know the etiquette.

Chelsea decided to stay inside. She replaced her cup on the coffee table and sat down in the middle of the couch. Through the open doorway came a rush of soft laughter from Kayako. A chirp from Grandmother. Muffled laughter from the men. Excited talk.

Again Chelsea felt the pangs of the outsider. Although she was sure they would include her as much as they could, still she knew she wasn't part of this culture and never would be. Not so for Yoshi. In a short time he had managed to ease into his family's connections.

With a sigh, Chelsea fingered her cup. It would be impossible to relate the way Yoshi did, even with her own family. She had cut all ties the year she went away to college, no longer willing to watch her mother and father drinking and hurting each other, not wanting to be a witness to their pain.

She stood up and then sat down again, feeling it best to wait for explanations. First, she must present herself, even if her bangs looked a mess and her lipstick was gone. She straightened her jacket and took off her hat, setting it on the arm of the couch.

Again Chelsea stood as one by one they came through the doorway, smiles wide, eyes briefly on her, then lowered, as if to look at her another moment might make her uncomfortable. Only Yoshi, the last to enter, stared openly. "Grandmother and Toru," he said, "this is my friend, Chelsea Jarvis. *She walks in beauty, like the night.*"

Grandmother looked up in surprise.

Yoshi laughed self-consciously and blushed. He inspected his well-polished shoes as if they might give him assistance. "That's from a famous poem by Keats," he said. "It, ah, well, it popped into my head."

"That was lovely, Yoshi, " Chelsea said, resisting an impulse to rush over and hug him. Imagine, introducing her in such a poetic manner. Perhaps he hadn't slipped into their culture. Maybe he had invented his own.

Grandmother's mouth twitched. She said to Yoshi, "Poetry good when 'popped.' What about haiku? Sometimes I haiku make. You do?"

"No, I...I don't write poetry." He added lamely, "I quote what other people write."

"That also good," remarked Grandmother. She said to Chelsea, "Come, come, please sit."

Chelsea obeyed and Grandmother sat on the couch beside her, lighting as delicately as a butterfly on a leaf.

"I hope everything went okay for you at the airport," said Chelsea. "What you did was pretty amazing."

"A mosquito's teardrop," Grandmother replied.

They all laughed and Grandmother clapped her hands.

"My sincere thanks," Chelsea said. "I really appreciate the rescue."

Grandmother patted Chelsea's arm. "Our American relative we must help. You Tsuyoshi's friend. Both long way from home."

Everyone nodded and smiled. Toru set his bundle down on the kitchen counter and went into the bedroom to hang up his jacket. Pulling a white chair away from the white table, Great Uncle Nagata sank down with a sigh.

"Now," said Grandmother, leaning forward, "secret envelope, you open."

"I don't know." Chelsea bit her lower lip. "To open this sealed correspondence is a breach of contract with my client."

"Who's your client?" asked Yoshi. "Eric or Mr. Hayashi?"

Toru came back into the room. "I don't think it matters which man is Chelsea's client. From what Yoshi told me, both men got her into lots of trouble. Neither deserve consideration."

Chelsea looked at Yoshi, at Grandmother, at the other three faces. Could she trust them? They seemed honest and helpful. She had to believe they'd continue to help her. What else could she do?

"Eric was my client," she said to Yoshi. "However, you're right, Toru. Not only did he deceive me, but he forced me into a relationship with criminals. I consider the contract with him broken."

She unlatched her briefcase, pulled out the manila envelope and ran a thumb over the imprinted red peony. Slipping a fingernail under the envelope flap, she cracked the wax seal open.

The room was silent, serious looks on all faces.

CHAPTER 19

From the manila envelope, Chelsea pulled out a thin, red silk package. Attached to the top was a piece of paper with Japanese writing on it. She handed it to Toru. "What does this say?"

"*Shashin*. That's Japanese for photograph, followed by 'MO' written in English capital letters. *Heya* is room. And then the number 512, followed by *Doyobi, Sungatsu Jushichi-nichi*, Japanese for Saturday, March 17. Last on here is '0200'—two in the morning." Toru handed the paper to Yoshi, who set it on the white table for Great Uncle Nagata to read.

Chelsea untied the gold cord binding the silk package. In it were five, eight by ten photographs. A quick glance at the first one took her breath away: two naked men in bed having sex. Her hands no longer felt attached to her arms. This wasn't what she had expected. No securities. No money. No special instructions. No secret formulas. All five photographs were of different sexual acts performed in bed by the same two men.

Grandmother peered over at the photos. "Oh, oh, they in the act," she whispered.

Chelsea looked up at Yoshi. "Pretty weird, hey?"

Yoshi winced as he glanced through the five pictures. "My God, no privacy here. He handed the photos to Toru who gave a low whistle and spread them out on the white table.

Great Uncle Nagata's eyebrows shot up as he surveyed the pictures. "Hm-m-m," he said, seeming more curious than shocked, "one man is Japanese, the other Caucasian." He studied the piece of paper. "These photographs were taken at the MO in room 512 at two a.m. on Saturday, March 17. I bet 'MO' stands for a place—a city or a hotel."

"Mandarin Orange?" Kayako said thoughtfully. "It big, fancy hotel." She peered at one of the photos, covered her mouth and sat down next to Grandmother as if wiser to keep her distance.

Toru nodded. "The Mandarin Orange. Yeah, that makes sense."

"Recognize either of the guys?" Chelsea asked him.

Toru shook his head.

Yoshi picked up one of the photographs from the table. "Not positive, but I believe the Caucasian man is a U.S. Congressman. Can't think of his name and don't know which state he's from. But if it's him, he's a guy who touts family values—a staunch right-winger."

Grandmother wrinkled her nose. "Two wings better for flying."

Great Uncle Nakata said, "The Japanese man in these pictures looks familiar. Pretty sure in our House of Councilors."

"Obviously, there's a plan," said Yoshi, "to blackmail at least one of these men. I imagine whoever is the richest and most influential."

"The American Congressman," said Chelsea, fingering the silk wrapping, "since the package was headed for the United States."

Toru frowned. "But why did they feel it necessary to sneak this envelope into America? Nothing illegal about mailing photographs or carrying them through customs."

"Unless, the yakuza stole them from Japanese government files," said Yoshi.

Great Uncle Nagata added, "The Japanese Secret Service may have heard about the theft of the photographs and feared they might create an international incident."

"If Grandfather is correct," Toru said, "they may be searching for these photos, checking all avenues to the U.S. including snail and electronic mail."

"And," said Yoshi, "if they know or even suspect a yakuza syndicate has them, they would search any yakuza member going through customs."

"Also they may know about Eric's connection and would search him," Chelsea said. She stood up, her eyes narrowing as she stared at the envelope. "I imagine he's been laundering funds for the yakuza ever since I formed his company."

Abruptly, Toru locked the front door with a resounding click, startling the others. "So, not only yakuza hunting for you," he said to Chelsea, "but Secret Service if they learn what you have."

Chelsea dropped the silk cloth and cord on the photos as if they were all too hot. "Let's just call the Secret Service and give them everything."

Toru shook his head. "If you knew the right person to call, fine, but some in the yakuza may have strings to certain operatives. Better first to investigate."

Grandmother spoke up. "My husband, the good people can locate. May take time. He busy man in Tokyo. But he help. I make sure."

With the others watching, Chelsea gathered the photos together, rewrapped them in the silk cloth, tied on the cord and reattached the piece of paper on top. She slipped the bundle into the envelope and swallowed hard. "What should I do with this envelope? Can't keep it, Refuse to deliver it to Eric. Leery of giving it to the police. I could tear up the photos and throw them away but probably Hayashi has copies, and that wouldn't stop the yakuza from hunting me down and taking revenge."

"I have no idea what to do," Yoshi said, throwing up his hands.

The room was silent, serious looks on all faces.

At last, Grandmother piped up. "No decisions until we eat."

"Grandmother's right," said Toru. "We can think better if not hungry. He opened his parcel on the kitchen counter and distributed a paper-wrapped box to each person. "On the way home I bought *bento*." He explained to Chelsea, "Japanese fast food."

Kayako covered her mouth, suppressing a giggle. "Tsuyoshi's grandmother not let him buy hamburgers at McDonalds."

113

"Burgers bad for body," stated Grandmother and everyone smiled.

"*Chotto,*" said Kayako, hurrying to the kitchen. "I make more tea."

Grandmother called a stream of Japanese after her, Chelsea picking out some of the words—instructions for which tea to use, how much, something about the temperature.

"*Hai, hai,*" Kayako kept saying.

Grandmother peeked up at Yoshi, who remained standing by one of the white chairs. Her eyes grew brighter and she cocked her head to one side like a bird. Raising her arms, she burst out in flute tones what seemed like a Japanese poem.

Chelsea was enthralled. "Sounds beautiful. Unfortunately, I haven't a clue what you said."

"It's a famous haiku," Yoshi said quietly. Looking at Grandmother, he translated:

Wake up! Wake up!
I'll make of thee my comrade
Sleeping butterfly.

With a gay laugh Grandmother clasped her hands on her chest. "Tsuyoshi understands haiku by Basho." She lowered her head. "You see, I too can pop poetry."

CHAPTER 20

"You and Tsuyoshi must hide," Grandmother said to Chelsea. She piled up the empty bento boxes and carried them to the sink. "Hide until...until all blows over." She turned around and rolled her eyes.

"Blows over?" Yoshi was continually amazed at Grandmother's slang. "Okay, we hide, but where?"

"I have good idea," Grandmother answered. "Toru?" She bowed to him. "Your iPhone, please."

Grandmother took the phone into the bedroom. After a short conversation, she returned and announced, "All is fixed. You go to countryside. Other side of Honshu. To my son's house."

"Uncle Iiyama's?" said Yoshi, shocked. "We can't stay with my mother's brother."

"Why not?" asked Chelsea.

"He was terribly upset when she married an American and moved from Japan.

"But that was years ago. Surely he's gotten over that."

"I doubt it. He's never written to her, although my father said she wrote many letters to him. She never heard from her father either. He also opposed the marriage. Doubt if either of them would welcome me."

Grandmother patted Yoshi's arm, "Your Uncle Iiyama says yes you come stay. He say, '*Dekirudake tetsudai shimas.*'"

"He will assist as much as he can," Yoshi translated to Chelsea.

After wetting he lips, Grandmother added, "As for your grandfather—he means good. He has big job in Tokyo, so not available for us." She chuckled. "Even I, his wife, do not see him much."

Yoshi knew how difficult it was in this culture to say *no*. Easier to pretend with a *yes* and, if that wasn't meant, find a way to make it a *no* without confrontation. Probably his uncle didn't want him, but felt he had to say *yes*. With a sigh, Yoshi sat down in one of the white chairs and hung his head.

He remembered asking his father about the relatives in Japan. "The only one I met was your grandmother," his father had said. "A wonderful lady, mischievous sense of humor, kind heart. The rest refused to meet me. Your Great Uncle Nagata might have agreed to the marriage but he was in Singapore at the time. He's made a number of phone calls to us, insisting we should come to Japan and visit them. Your mother didn't want to go back, her hurt was too deep. Unfortunately, because she married me, she lost her people."

When Yoshi tried to speak to his mother about this, she refused to talk about it. "Best forgotten," she had said, looking through the kitchen window as though her past might be drifting around in the backyard. With an abrupt sweep of her hands, she left Yoshi with the notion that her previous life was not to be discussed.

Shortly after that, Yoshi began to frequent Japanese restaurants, take language courses, practice Japanese sentences with recordings, attempt to speak Japanese with exchange students, listen to koto music. Still, he didn't feel Japanese. Following the break up with Evelyn, he immersed his spare time in studies of Japanese culture until he thought if he had known more about it as a teenager, he might have ended up in the Department of Asian Languages and Literature. Not that he disliked being an English Literature professor or his field of expertise. He relished the Romantic Age, identified with the images and thoughts of many of its writers.

Acknowledging himself as the only Japanese link left in his American family, he had decided to go to Japan to see if the chain might be restored. He had been warmly welcomed in Japan except for his grandfather, who said he didn't have time to meet him, and Uncle Iiyama, who didn't seem enthused to see him. Had he now agreed only because his mother had insisted?

Grandmother tapped Yoshi on the head. "Sit up straight, Grandson. We must do big thinking."

A twinge of anxiety shot through Yoshi along with a desire to retreat back into his poetry world. However, setting his jaw firmly, he rose and said, "Yes, of course." He hurried into the bedroom and from his suitcase dug out a map. Returning, he unfolded it on the white table. "Uncle Iiyama lives in a remote area on the other side of Honshu," he told Chelsea. "It's the perfect place for us to hide." What Yoshi didn't say was he thought barging into Uncle Iiyama's as a fugitive with another American, a woman lawyer, and begging for help was not the best way to bridge the chasm between him and his uncle.

Yoshi straightened his back. "Great Uncle Nagata, could you take us to the Odawara train station? There we can take the Shinkansen to Okayama where we pick up the train to Matsue."

"*Hai, hai,*" cried Great Uncle Nagata.

Toru said, "I'll go with you. In case anyone is watching your actions, I'll purchase your tickets all the way to Matsue."

"Good."

Chelsea came over for a look at the map. "I gather Matsue is the closest city to where your Uncle Iiyama lives."

"Yes, I checked this out a year ago when I first had the idea of visiting Japan."

She put on her reading glasses. "Looks as if the city's located on the Sea of Japan."

"Close to it," said Yoshi. "Actually it's on Lake Shinji."

"Never heard of Matsue."

"Not an American tourist mecca," said Toru. "Takes a hunk of time to reach the east side of Honshu, and there's so much to see on this western side." He leaned over to study the map. "This is how you'll travel." He pointed to places on the map as he talked. "First you take a Bullet Train from Odawara to Okayama. There you change to the Yakumo Limited Express that winds through this mountain pass to Matsue."

Yoshi said, "If it's all right with Uncle Iiyama, we'll stay with him for a week. It'll give us time to decide what to do next. Review all our options."

Grandmother said, "Your Uncle Iiyama said he meet you near drawbridge to old feudal castle."

Kayako spoke up. "Bronze tiger on our front gate from him."

Grandmother nodded. "It gift for Toru when young boy."

"Why a tiger?" Chelsea asked.

Grandmother pursed her lip. "You go there. You understand."

"Better leave your laptop, briefcase and suitcase here," Toru said to Chelsea. "They identify you. No problem with your suitcase Yoshi. We can decide later how, when and where to ship Chelsea's stuff."

Grandmother said, "I have another idea. Matter of safety. Chelsea, you tall lady. You too easy to see. Better you dress like a man." She eyed Chelsea's ample breasts. "Also, bind chest. Make flat."

Kayako giggled and hid her face in her hands. Great Uncle Nagata laughed.

Chelsea grinned and said, "Good idea. Yoshi I'm going to borrow some of your clothes for a dress rehearsal"

Hurrying into the bedroom, she changed into a pair of Yoshi's slacks, one of his sport shirts and his crew-necked sweater. Great Uncle Nagata lent her shoes, which fit, to everyone's surprise but Chelsea. Toru gave her a baseball cap. Kayako contributed dark glasses and reminded her to take off her earrings. Chelsea removed her makeup and nail polish, clipped her nails short, and tucked her bangs up under the cap.

Yoshi scarcely recognized her. She looked like a young man. Noticing how fondly she caressed her black hat before handing it to Kayako, he said, "Don't worry. They'll ship it back to you along with your suitcase."

"Not necessary," she replied. "I can buy another one. I'd like to keep this, though." She removed the gold CJ from the bowler and pinned it inside the baseball cap.

Grandmother held up the fiber bag she had used in the airport rescue. "Here. New suitcase."

"Perfect," said Chelsea. She placed the manila envelope along with her passport and iPhone in the bottom of the bag. Searching through her suitcase, she came up with changes of socks, underwear and shirts, stuffing them into the bag.

Later, after the lights were out and all had retired to their futons, Yoshi smiled, remembering how Chelsea looked as she practiced various masculine moves and gestures and tried to deepen her voice. What were his true feelings about this woman? Was it love? Didn't that take time to cultivate? A period to find mutual understandings, common ground, respect for each other's ideas? Was it then only physical attraction?

No, more than that. He treasured her spirit, respected her courage, her intelligence, cherished her humor. He was amazed at her ability to handle people like Hayashi and Kagawa.

She affected him physically in ways he found embarrassing. A glance at her, sitting on the couch, leaning over the map on the kitchen table, standing before him in her disguise, excited him. He longed to take her in his arms and race up the slopes of Mt. Fuji. To grasp her hand and run into a fierce gale. To make love with her in a drenching storm. To float beside her on a warm lake under a cloak of stars. Seeded dreams that rose to the surface ready to sprout.

He looked at the bedroom door barely visible in the darkness. Was she wearing a nightgown? Did she sleep curled up or stretched out. On her stomach? On her back? On her side? A hot current raced through him. He pictured her on her left side. Naked. Half curled. Right leg stretched out. Left cheek resting on a cupped hand. He struggled to switch off his thoughts, think in other directions. He pushed off the cover and wiped his damp face with the back of a hand. You came to Japan to visit relatives, he told himself. Let it rest. Instead, meditate on yesterday's tea ceremony.

He had made it through the two-hour rite in Grandmother's tea house without a major blunder, kneeling beside Grandmother. Great Uncle Nagata's movements were easy yet precise as he performed the duties of tea master. The quiet beauty, the utter concentration, the process of sharing the tea, everything about the ceremony brought peace to his body, even though at the conclusion he could barely stand and his knees still ached.

These people were good. He liked his family here in Japan, admired their commitment to stick together, to help each other. Family ties were important. Not that his bonds with them were complete. They never would be. Only their exteriors were connected, their interiors likely different from his. Yet, he felt closer to his family here, especially to Grandmother, than to his family at home, whom he dearly loved and who loved him.

So far in his life, the physical touching of humans had not been something often experienced. Evelyn had been more of an intellectual partner. Oh, they had slept together once a week for a year, but somehow it seemed a methodical act, an expected situation, nothing ever said of love. The only other relationship had been that summer when he was eighteen. She had returned to Princeton that fall, hadn't answer his letter and he'd lost track of her.

Why was it all so different with Chelsea?

Warmth spread throughout his body, not fast and hot—more of a comfortable glow that filled his corners and allowed his muscles to relax, images fading out like colors from a sunset.

CHAPTER 21

They boarded the Bullet Train in Odawara, Chelsea before Yoshi, who scrutinized each entrant to their car before leaping on moments before the train left the station. He performed the same act of caution when they took the train from Okayma to Matsue. This time, however, he felt more nervous as the ride would be longer and to their final destination.

Pulling his roll-on suitcase behind him, he sauntered down the aisle, checking for a vacant seat. He sat in the row behind Chelsea—separate travelers. When he snapped his suitcase handle down, he momentarily felt the appraising eyes of the passengers.

During the ride to Matsue, Yoshi alternated between relaxation and high alert. The train wound through a mountain pass that reminded him of the Cascades at home. At one point, he grew so mesmerized by trees rising out of rocky cliffs that he fell asleep. Ten minutes later, he woke up with a start, guilty, darting looks about to make certain no threat existed. Satisfied, he allowed himself to doze off again. Only to awaken once more, every muscle in his body tense.

No reason to be afraid, he assured himself, disgusted with his nervousness. Chelsea was safe, disguised as a young man;

the passengers seemed engrossed in their own worlds. Since he hadn't slept much last night, too keyed up, too many thoughts swirling, he concluded it was wise to use this time to rest so he could handle whatever problems might lie ahead.

Once more he glanced at the passengers. Faces more open than those of canny Tokyoites, an at-ease-with-the-world look here, an acceptance of life. A few elderly women wore kimonos, others in smocks and head scarves. The younger women wore Western-style dresses or slacks. All of the men had on sport shirts and dark trousers; no suits or ties. It pleased him to see how well he fit into this landscape.

From the seat across the aisle, a young man sprang up. Yoshi's stomach twitched. The young man stood soldier-like before Chelsea.

"I student!" the young man proclaimed. "English I practice. Excuse me. You American?"

"Yeah," said Chelsea in a surprisingly deep voice.

Yoshi stomach settled down. He was fascinated by Chelsea's mannish way of acting—hunched down, hands in pockets, right foot resting on left thigh.

The young man bowed his head to her. "My name Eiichi. Your name?"

"Bob," Chelsea replied, "from Napa Valley, California. Raise grapes for a winery. We make a fine Cabernet Sauvignon." She turned away and stared out the window at the scenery.

The student turned to Yoshi and addressed him in Japanese.

Yoshi's mouth felt full of sawdust. Again his stomach jumped around. At first he thought of answering in Japanese, passing himself off as a local. He decided his accent would give him away. After swallowing hard a few times, he managed to speak.

"I'm Bill Nakata. I...uh...I work for General Motors in Detroit. I'm one of their executives."

"Ah, auto ex-e-cu-tive," the young man said carefully.

"Yes, indeed. Our plant builds Cadillacs. Excellent cars. Of course, the companies here in Japan also make good cars. I suppose you can tell I'm an American. However, my parents were born in Kyoto and I speak some Japanese. Enough to get along."

Yoshi was amazed at how easily his story was rolling out. In a macho manner he continued, "I'm headed for Matsue to confer with a group from Toyota."

The student's eyes widened. "In Matsue?"

Realizing the meeting probably would have occurred in Tokyo, Yoshi said quickly, "Right, well, we're all on holiday." Enough of this, he decided, his ground feeling rockier by the word. "Well..." Yoshi inserted a tone of cheerfulness. "Nice talking to you. Enjoy your train ride." He feigned weariness and leaned back, closing his eyes, cautiously opening them a few minutes later. To his relief the student was back in his seat, reading a book.

Yoshi surveyed the passenger car to see if anything suspicious was happening. A man turned away from his gaze and began to clean his glasses with his handkerchief, and a middle-aged man three rows back frowned. Embarrassed to be caught staring, Yoshi faced front not wanting to be considered a crude foreigner. He looked at the aisle floor, littered with paper wrappers, cardboard lunch boxes, empty bottles and plastic cups. The Japanese might consider him a crude foreigner, but he wasn't a litterbug. He felt like running about to pick it all up. Mustn't do anything to attract attention. Besides, it probably gives a job to a cleanup person.

Two hours later the train arrived in Matsue. Chelsea grabbed her fiber bag and hurried down the aisle. As Yoshi started to follow, the aisle began to fill up with people exiting rows in front of him. Realizing it would be impolite to push his way past, he decided to wait for them to move on. Why were they taking so long to gather up their belongings?

Slowly they filed out, row by row, one by one in an orderly procession, nodding, bowing, smiling, progress at a creep. Yoshi hid his agitation by examining the handle on his suitcase. In Tokyo, fast had been the norm, lines in subway or train stations flowing like rivers. Here people moved like a trickling stream.

At last he reached the platform, where a cool breeze off Lake Shinji broke the warmth of the sun. Chelsea, dark glasses on, stood in front of the station as if waiting for someone. He debated whether he should join her now or wait until the passengers dispersed. Best to wait.

The student approached him and chattered in a mix of English and Japanese. He said his friend was picking him up.

They would be happy to give Yoshi a ride to wherever his hotel was.

Chelsea moved away from the depot and walked down the street.

"*Dono hoteru?*" the student asked Yoshi. "You my Japanese understand?"

Yoshi's eyes followed Chelsea. Then he realized the student was talking to him. "What?" He blinked. "Oh, my hotel. Well, I'm not sure which one it is. The Toyota people made all the arrangements. I'm off to meet them now." He started after Chelsea.

"Wait," the student cried. "Here my friend." He indicated a car driving up to the station. "We help."

"No, no, I need the exercise. Anyway, it's not far. *Arigato.*" Yoshi strode off. Remembering his manners, he turned back and bowed.

He no longer saw Chelsea. She must have taken the street to the right. It led north toward Matsue Castle where they were to meet Uncle Iiyama. The castle sat on the hill like an old giant brooding over the city.

The southern section of town was a mix of cubed, commercial buildings and new houses, the streets empty. Since it was early afternoon, Yoshi surmised women were involved in household duties, children in school, men at work, older folks taking naps. He walked beside what looked like a canal, bridges crossing at intervals. Between two houses, he glimpsed the silver blue of Lake Shinji.

Still no sign of Chelsea. He wished for a bottle of ice cold green tea to quiet his insides.

A car slowly approached from the rear as if its occupants were looking for someplace or someone. Yoshi tensed.

The car stopped beside him.

It was the student and his friend. With a solemn face, the student nodded to Yoshi, who, attempting to look casual, nodded back. The car moved on down the street.

Had it been an insult not to accept the student's invitation for a ride? Should he not have closed his eyes and feigned sleep on the train, continuing the conversation instead? Was the story about being an auto executive a big mistake?

Most likely he thought the answer was yes to all of these questions. He wanted to do what was correct, didn't want to seem a callous, bumbling gaijin, but he didn't see how he could always say and do the right thing, bowing and catering to everyone he met in Japan. There were problems to consider, a tenuous situation to handle.

To hell with conformity! No matter how hard I try, I can't do everything right over here. Relationships in Japan are too structured, too formal, too many chances to go wrong, too difficult to know what might offend.

He rounded the corner. There was Chelsea, the car stopped, the student talking to her. Yoshi turned around and pretended to examine the bark on a tree. The car drove on. Chelsea glanced back, then continued forward. He followed, keeping the same distance between them.

Three girls in white blouses and black skirts, black caps on their heads, emerged from what might be a schoolhouse and stood in the gateway, giggling. They shouted at Chelsea. "Hi, Mister." "You American?" "You like Japan?" "Want to take our picture?" "You awesome guy." "Bye, bye."

Chelsea waved and walked faster.

As Yoshi approached, one of the girls whistled. More giggles. Another girl blew him a kiss. They all laughed uproariously and waved their caps at him. Yoshi felt his face turn red. Although he sometimes found Japanese traditions difficult to understand, modern Japanese ways confused him even more. He kept on walking, staring at his shoes, his suitcase clattering on behind him like a reluctant child, until the girls were behind him. When he looked up, Chelsea was gone again. He spurted ahead, but didn't see her. Had she turned up a side road? He looked around then raced on, reaching a canal with a number of bridges. Which one had she taken? Again he reminded himself she couldn't get lost. Their destination was always visible—the fortress castle on the hill, surrounded by a gray stone wall, a moat of water linked to the lake. With each step, the five-story towers of the keep looked more forbidding. The series of black-tiled, sloping roofs gave them a hooded look, and the dark open gateway to the ground floor of the *donjon*, as the keep was called, resembled a gaping mouth.

He hurried on, his heart pounding. Nothing must happen to Chelsea. What if yakuza agents recognized her and picked her up, kidnapped her again? Impossible. Her disguise was too good. They couldn't know she was here in Matsue.

To calm his fears, Yoshi took deep breaths and muttered phrases about the castle from Lafcadio Hearn's 1890 book: "*Crested at its summit, like a feudal helmet...two colossal fishes....*" He looked up and saw them in bronze. "*Bristling with horned gables and gargoyled eaves.*" Hearn had not been just another gaijin for he found a way to become a part of this culture.

Houses in the northern section of the city looked more traditional, older. Unpainted, weathered wooden structures surrounded by trees and gardens. Newly-leafed branches arched over narrow streets that twisted up and away from what appeared to be the main road to the castle.

As he walked up the hill—Kameda Hill he remembered from the tour book—he met a few people on the street, friendly, polite, nodding. By a garden gate, two women, each balancing a quilted cradle on her chest, chatted and laughed, while their babies peeked out, observing the world with eyes like shiny black marbles. An elderly man in a kimono stood in his garden, smiling serenely at a cherry tree—a cloud of pink blossoms. Could yakuza thugs or government secret service operatives infiltrate these lives? They would be more out of place in this setting than he.

There. At last. Chelsea. Beside the moat, staring into the water. Good grief, she must have found a short cut or else run all the way. He decided not to go up to her now. Find Uncle Iiyama first.

A man wearing glasses stood on the drawbridge inspecting the castle gateway; Yoshi thought he had seen him on the train. Another man leaned against the wall that encircled the moat. He looked in his early sixties and wore a loose-fitting, belted, white shirt and baggy, navy blue shorts that reached his knees, on his head a conical straw hat, the kind Yoshi remembered seeing in Hiroshige prints. On his feet were wooden clogs about two inches high. His face looked like carved ivory, the old kind, darkened with age. Straggles of gray hair curved around the sides of his upper lip and dipped down to meet a thin beard that hung from his chin to the middle of his chest. Yoshi searched for a resemblance to his mother. The eyes and the shape of the cheekbones looked the same. He walked over to the man.

"Uncle Iiyama?"

The man nodded. "Tsuyoshi?" he whispered with the sound of the wind.

"Yes."

At that moment, a group of tourists, led by a tour guide who spoke French, poured from a bus and headed for the bridge. The throng paused, huddling around the guide for further instructions.

Uncle Iiyama beckoned for Yoshi to follow him, then clopped past the tour group and along the street that edged the moat, his clogs on the pavement sounding like hoof beats.

Yoshi skirted the tourists, studying each face, concluding they were what they seemed. He looked back. Chelsea walked a few yards behind him. In this manner they followed Uncle Iiyama until they arrived at an ox-drawn cart loaded in the middle with bulging white sacks. At the driver's end of the cart was a heavy-paper bag that reeked of fertilizer, next to it bucket that smelled like fish. At the far end, a crate of live chickens.

Uncle Iiyama, with surprisingly agile moves, clambered into the cart where he rearranged the sacks, setting them into two flat piles. "*Gohan*" he informed Yoshi. With elbow and head jerks, he indicated they should climb aboard and sit on the sacks.

The situation astonished Yoshi so much that for a few moments he was unable to say or do anything. On the train, they had cautiously traveled like strangers. In town they had walked vigilantly, keeping a distance between them. Now, they were supposed to climb atop an oxcart and sit together on sacks of rice, surrounded by fertilizer, a smelly bucket, and a crate of chickens. In this manner they would clatter through the streets of Matsue. What would the student and his friend think if they saw the General Motors' executive and the Napa Valley grape grower, side by side on an oxcart? If the yakuza or the government agents came to Matsue and inquired about foreigners, the locals could inform them about this unusual sighting.

Uncle Iiyama kept gesturing for Yoshi and Chelsea to get up on the rice. Apparently he didn't realize Yoshi understood Japanese, because in that language he used a few potent expletives and stated that by the time they got into the cart, the eels would be dead.

Uncle Iiyama didn't look like any Japanese men Yoshi had seen or read about in today's Japan. But, then he realized he didn't know much about country people. His uncle could be quite normal for where he lived, although Yoshi doubted it. And an ox cart in Japan? Unheard of these days.

Chelsea clambered onto the cart and sat on the rice bags.

Yoshi handed her the fiber bag and the suitcase and then pulled himself over the railing.

The uncle grunted approvingly and rubbed his chin with the back of a hand.

Yoshi muttered to Chelsea, "I don't like the idea of riding up here, exposed to the sky, with a clopping ox and a bunch of squawking chickens announcing our approach."

"I know." She peered into the pail. "My God, there's something live in there."

"Eels," said Yoshi, "and that stuff is fertilizer, and those chickens don't look happy, so I wouldn't get near their beaks. It appears this was my uncle's shopping day in town."

She held her nose.

Uncle Iiyama reached under his driving seat board and pulled out a large, black blanket. He waved his arms indicating they should lie down. They obeyed and he threw the blanket over them.

Peeking out from under the edge, Yoshi saw his uncle untie the reins from a tree, scramble onto his board seat and, with a sharp cry, slap the reins. The cart jerked forward, wooden wheels squeaking against the pavement like an old door. They bounced and creaked down a narrow, cobbled street.

"Chelsea, are you okay?" Yoshi asked.

She peered out from the other edge of the blanket. "Fine, fine," she replied, suppressing a laugh. "But I don't think we're in Japan any more."

At the bottom of the hill, they headed north, the castle of Matsue, looking more and more like a harmless toy.

CHAPTER 22

Chelsea's shoulder muscles felt tight, her mouth dry. The smell from the fertilizer and the eels was overpowering. She considered scooting to the other end of the rice sacks but realized she would have to put up with the chickens. She heard a voice pass along the street. Another voice. Two children jabbering and what sounded like a ball bouncing.

The cart jerked to a stop. She peeked out. They were at a T-intersection, a scattering of people, some carrying loads, walked along the sides of a straight road. A bicycle churned by. A car sputtered up behind them. She hid her head and listened to it pass. The cart turned left.

The road was smoother now, not as much jolting. After a while she looked out and sniffed. The odor didn't seem as bad. Cautiously, she uncovered her head, relieved to see the road empty. Rice paddies stretched to the east, a lagoon to the west, mountains to the north. Matsue was barely visible to the south, the top of the castle floating in a mist—a beautiful scene. The ride was turning into something enjoyable: jostling along with Yoshi atop rice sacks though picturesque Japan. Her edginess disappeared. She felt ridiculously like a school girl and wondered why and how it had happened.

She sat up. "Come out, come out, wherever you are," she called to Yoshi and pinched his arm.

With a snort, Yoshi threw back the blanket, sat up and met her eyes.

She squirmed around to kneel facing forward on the rice bags, one arm holding onto the side railing. Yoshi knelt beside her. They alternately studied the landscape and each other until, unable to resist the temptation, she hugged him with her free arm. He hugged her back. They laughed and he hugged her with both arms and she did the same. They continued to kneel that way, bouncing along together, laughing.

Uncle Iiyama peered back at them as if they were from another planet.

She supposed she should feel embarrassed, but she didn't. As they rode along, holding on to each other, she forgot the yakuza, the manila envelope, Eric, even forgot she was a lawyer. She was young Chelsea, kneeling beside a man she liked, their arms entwined, enjoying the ride in Uncle Iiyama's primitive cart, wishing it would go on forever.

A bus loomed on the horizon, barreling toward them. She watched its progress as if her eyes were magnetized. The bus closed in. Uncle Iiyama shouted a warning. They let go of each other and ducked down, heads between knees like school children preparing for an earthquake drill. With a jerk the cart veered off the road. The chickens squawked and flopped, feathers flew. Water from the fish bucket splashed onto Yoshi's legs. He fell against Chelsea. She grabbed the railing to steady herself. The oxcart executed a tight circle to face the road, stopping on a narrow strip of ground elevated between two rice paddies.

Uncle Iiyama turned around and snapped, *"Kakure."*

Chelsea and Yoshi yanked the blanket over them and flattened down, facing each other

Goosebumps rose on Chelsea's arms.

The bus slowed down.

"It's all right," Yoshi reassured her. "It's only because the road's narrow."

The bus crept past and then picked up speed again, the sound of its engine fading away. The ox pulled the cart back onto the road, wheels creaking, chickens clucking.

Yoshi threw back the blanket. His eyes had the look of a burglar caught in the act. He cradled Chelsea's face with his hands, leaned over and kissed her tenderly.

She threw her arms around his neck, pulled him down beside her and kissed him hard.

At that moment, the cart hit the road bump and the fertilizer bag bounced in the air, spewing some of its contents on Yoshi's head. With a gasp he scrambled up, brushing himself off.

Chelsea laughed. Yoshi joined in. Even Uncle Iiyama seemed amused. He shouted back something unintelligible and chortled as he slapped the reins.

An hour later the cart again turned off the main road, this time onto a dirt lane toward the mountains. They passed more rice paddies. Then they rattled into the foothills through a grove of stunted conifers that had the scent of rosin.

The ox broke into a jerky gallop. The cart careened around a group of rocks that jutted up like spires, steam rising from a large pool at their base. A thatch-roofed house appeared, walls of shoji screens interspersed with unpainted wood, the porch railing covered with wisteria. Clusters of purple flowers hung from the vine like miniature grapes.

"*Watashi no uchi!*" cried Uncle Iiyama, pointing to his house. He laughed and let go of the reins. The animal raised its head and bellowed as it lumbered around to the rear, bouncing the cart past a shed that might have been a barn, toward another building which, except for its roof appendages—a bubble skylight at one end and a screened section at the other—had the appearance of an old warehouse: long, windowless, weathered wood sides and double doors, one side open. Attached to the closed door was a fierce tiger head made of bronze, larger than the one on the front gate to the Odawara house.

The ox stopped before the open doorway. The animal tossed its head and stamped its hooves, snorting impatiently.

Uncle Iiyama jumped down and waved for Yoshi and Chelsea to get out of the cart. He removed the fish pail and the crate of squawking chickens with great arcing motions. Then he clopped off into the building, balancing the crate on his shoulder, swinging the pail, yelling a torrent of Japanese.

Chelsea slipped to the ground. Yoshi handed her the fiber bag then clambered out with his suitcase. A cacophony of voices floated from the building, all speaking Japanese.

Chelsea looked questioningly at Yoshi.

He shrugged. "Can't understand what they're saying—too fast, words overlapping, a country dialect I think."

"Maybe they don't want us here."

"Maybe they don't."

She took off her cap and ran her fingers through her bangs, trying to bring some order. "Bet I look a mess."

He smiled. "You look great."

She tossed her billed cap into the fiber bag. It no longer seemed necessary to wear a hat. She could manage without it.

The ox bellowed again.

Only Uncle Iiyama could be heard now, his voice ringing out through the doorway. Then, laughter burst from the others inside. Chelsea imagined Uncle Iiyama telling about his passengers' love making being interrupted by the bag of fertilizer. Vigorously, she brushed Yoshi's hair. "Not a trace," she said.

"But my pants smell like eels," he replied, attempting to shake the wet side dry.

"If they're amused, that might make them friendly." She had the fleeting notion of waiting for a jury to render a decision.

A moment later, the other side of the warehouse double door shot open. A group of people stood, framed, as if ready for a photograph: two women in smocks—one young and pretty, the other with a streak of white hair that ran from the center of her forehead back to a tightly knotted bun; a man in his twenties, bare-chested, barefoot, wearing only a white loincloth, a head band, and leather mittens, goggles pushed to the top his head; an impish-looking boy about three who clutched a plastic ray gun; and Uncle Iiyama minus his straw hat, fish pail and chicken crate. All bowed in unison like actors taking a stage call.

Yoshi and Chelsea bowed back.

The two women erupted into a series of squeals, hiding their mouths with their hands.

The little boy pointed his toy ray gun at them and cried, *"Okashii, gaikokujin-kusai!"*

Yoshi blushed, his Adam's apple moving up and down.

A nervous chatter broke out among the doorway group. The younger woman grabbed the boy's free arm, and bowing and smiling, pulled him into the building. The other three closed ranks and bowed again.

As their faces resurfaced, they murmured a multitude of words, some Chelsea understood, like *"sumimasen"* and *"gomen nasai."* It seemed as if they were apologizing for what the boy had said. Well, nothing any of them did or said would affect her. It was important to appear cool and completely under control. People who showed they were influenced by how other people treated them inevitably got clobbered. Long ago she had learned to hide her emotions.

A zing of alarm shot through her. What about the display with Yoshi on the rice sacks? Had her carefully constructed cover lost a hinge?

"What did the kid say?" she whispered to Yoshi.

Scarcely moving his lips and staring straight ahead, he replied, "He thinks we're funny and foreign."

"We could say the same about them—a pretty weird scene here in Japan's back country. I'm beginning to understand how Alice felt when she crashed down the rabbit hole."

Deciding she must do something, she stepped forward and spoke in a pleasant but firm voice, "*Koko e mairimashita node ureshii desu.*" She wanted to let them know she was glad to be here. It was a sentence she had memorized on the plane, thinking she might use it with Hayashi only she hadn't felt that way when she met him.

Instant silence. Surprise on their faces. The nearly-naked man and the woman with the white-streaked hair looked at Uncle Iiyama. He pulled at his long mustache and gazed upward as if he expected something to drop from the sky.

After a tense moment, Uncle Iiyama came toward her with an outstretched hand. She took it, matching his soft grasp.

He smiled.

She smiled back.

"How do you do, Miss Jarvis," he said in heavily-accented English. "I trust there will be no problems here."

Chelsea couldn't believe her ears. She glanced back at Yoshi, who looked equally astonished.

"We—" Chelsea faltered. "We didn't realize you spoke English."

Uncle Iiyama's eyes gleamed as if he he'd caught a big fish. "For many years I taught art at the Tokyo University of Foreign Studies. I have only lived in the countryside for three years." He scratched his chin. "Although I am rusty with my English, when use becomes necessary, the rust wears away." He glanced sideways at Yoshi. "I don't forget things easily."

Yoshi cleared his throat and continued to stare as if his uncle had materialized from a genie's bottle.

Uncle Iiyama closed his eyes.

The silence accumulated.

Chelsea wondered if this was to make them feel uncomfortable or if he was clearing away the rust.

A stern look took over the old man's face. His eyes flew open. "Excuse me, Mr. Tsuyoshi Moore. I am happy your lady friend speaks a little Japanese. However, I should like to know about you. Do you speak only the words of an American?"

Yoshi wet his lips and then bowed low from the waist. *"Nihon-go wo honno sukoshi hanashimasu, ojisan."*

Uncle Iiyama dipped his head in acknowledgement and focused on Yoshi's Italian loafers. *"Jozu!"*

Holding the deep bow, Yoshi stared at Uncle Iiyama's wooden clogs.

"I did not believe," said Uncle Iiyama, "I would ever meet my sister's son."

Yoshi raised his head. "For many years I have wanted to meet my mother's brother."

"Your want is met. My disbelief is lost."

Again Yoshi's Adam's apple shot up and down. He straightened his back and said with a catch in his voice. "My mother sends you her love."

Uncle Iiyama looked away. At last he sighed and gestured for the two in the doorway to come forward. "This is my son, Shunsuke, and my wife, Ayako."

The inevitable bows followed.

He continued, "Inside you will meet Midori, my son's wife, and Hiro, their outspoken little boy."

The ox bellowed loudly, startling everyone.

"And that," said Uncle Iiyama with a sweeping gesture at the animal, "is our friend Rodosho, who sounds quite hungry." He turned to Shunsuke and spoke in rapid Japanese.

Shunsuke took off his mittens and quickly led the ox and cart away.

Inspecting Yoshi as if he were a rare specimen, Uncle Iiyama said, "*So desu.* Finally you have come to Japan to meet your relatives. By tomorrow we shall know if that was wise. Meanwhile, I bid you and your friend welcome." His smile took on a surprisingly paternal look.

He started for the doorway, calling back to them, "Come inside. You will see for yourself why this is called The Tiger House."

CHAPTER 23

Chelsea entered the warehouse after Uncle Iiyama, Yoshi followed. They stood by the doorway next to the crate of beady-eyed chickens and waited to be told what to do. Chelsea had the notion that as far as Uncle Iiyama was concerned there wasn't much difference between her and the chickens.

Late afternoon sun angled through the skylight, casting a soft light over the interior filled with orderly rows of tables—Chelsea counted ten, five to a side with a central aisle. Lined up on the tables, as if ready for a military drill, were papier-mâché tigers, about the size of new-born kittens. Each table held a different stage of completion: at the far end, partially-molded pieces; closest to the door, completed creatures—yellow with black stripes, heads bobbing from side to side on tiny pivots, angled tails fitted over stumps to hold them in place.

The head was the most individualistic part of each tiger, especially the mouth. Some hissed, jaws wide. Others snarled, lips curled ferociously. Still others laughed. All had gold eyes, above them blue geometric designs. Chelsea thought their stiff, nylon whiskers might have been been pulled from a scrub brush.

The building was divided in half, a wide doorway leading to the other part; Chelsea walked through it. The room was a foundry vented through a screened-in roof appendage. Attached to the pit by a long pipe was an air fan. Above the furnace, suspended on a crane, was a bucket-sized crucible. A metal pillar, perhaps an anvil, stood close to the furnace, as did a large metal box, possibly an oven near a sand pit. Hanging on a side wall, arranged in an orderly fashion, were hammers, mallets and lifting tongs. Shelves filled with boxes, bags and chunks of metal lined the back wall. Beside a plaster sand mold on a bench was what looked like a pouring shank; Chelsea remembered seeing a video of one holding a crucible of molten metal while pouring.

What caught her immediate attention was a bronze crouched tiger the size of a large house cat. It rested on a table in the center of the foundry room. So detailed was the animal, that when she first saw it she flinched, thinking it real. The head and shoulders of the animal glowed with a satin patina.

"I have not yet finished the polishing," said Uncle Iiyama, running a hand across the back of the cat in a caressing movement. "This piece was commissioned by a collector in India. It will be sent to him at the end of next week."

Yoshi murmured in admiration, "*Tiger! Tiger! Burning bright in the forests of the night.*"

"Ah, William Blake," cried Uncle Iiyama, his eyes lighting up.

"You've read Blake's poetry?" Yoshi asked in astonishment.

"I have attempted to read everything written about tigers. Not only in my language but in English, German, French and Chinese."

"Good heavens!" said Yoshi. He added quickly, "It is a beautiful work of art."

Uncle Iiyama inclined his head and smiled. "The bronze tiger is a joint venture. I make the wax model. My son does the foundry work. I clean, chase, polish and patina the piece."

Chelsea asked, "Excuse me, but do you mind my asking why your son goes barefoot and wears a loincloth?"

"He wishes to remain cool while he works."

"I should think he'd wear protective clothing. I mean, what if he gets too close to the furnace or accidentally spills molten metal? He could get badly burned."

"Shunsuke never gets burned and he never spills," replied Uncle Iiyama, bending his head to one side, his smile artificial. "He is careful."

Chelsea wondered if that was a put down. Did he mean *you might be sloppy but he isn't?* Or *Americans are but Japanese aren't?* Or did he only mean what he said. The uncle was so guarded with his words, so forced with his smile, she found it hard to tell what he thought.

Uncle Iiyama gestured toward the tables of papier-mâché tigers. "This side is run by my wife and daughter-in-law. Originally I designed the different heads, but now the ladies do everything from start to finish. My wife, Ayako, brings her good humor into making the tiny tigers, and Midori is a clever painter."

Chelsea examined a finished animal. "Cute little tigers."

Uncle Iiyama said, "Yes, these 'cute little tigers' are sold in Japan as collectible folk art."

Another put down? Chelsea wondered.

The two women sat on stools behind a table of unfinished tigers. They didn't seem to understand the English conversation. They whispered to each other and turned away to hide their smiles. Ayako's face was cheerfully wrinkled. Now and then, her streak of gray hair shone silver. Midori's skin was smooth and creamy and her hair, shiny as black satin, was partially hidden under a white bandanna tied at the back of her neck. Lit by the sun through the skylight, the women looked like a Renaissance painting.

A rustle from under the table. There knelt Hiro, his ray gun clutched in his hands. He peered out, a distrustful expression on his face.

Resisting a desire to stick out her tongue at the child, Chelsea ignored him and walked back to examine the bronze tiger. "Would you mind," she asked Uncle Iiyama, "if I asked a few more questions about your work?"

"Ask as you wish."

"Obviously you're a fine artist, yet it appears you concentrate only on tigers. How come?"

"When I was young," he replied, "I experimented, tried many mediums, explored numerous techniques. My most successful work, however, was in bronze animals."

He squinted at his sculpture as if analyzing its proportions. "In my country, Miss Jarvis, it is important to find ways to do things well. To seek perfection. I have learned how to create exceptionally fine animals. Refining the process further, I decided the tiger would be my trademark."

Her mind flashed to her bowler hat. "Trademarks are helpful," she said.

"I believe so."

"Why did you choose the tiger?"

"It is a symbol of courage, of fierce determination, of great strength—what we all want but seldom have, although at one time or another we pretend we do. *Tora no i o karu kitsune.* The fox assumes it is as fierce as a tiger." He chuckled, the sound much like the cluck of the hens now quiet in their cage.

"That saying," he continued, "is used about an underling who believes he has the power of his master."

"The tiger is furtive and cunning," she said. "It creeps about without a sound as it hunts for a victim."

"When a tiger needs a meal, do you expect it to play a drum to announce its presence?"

She shrugged. "If the tiger is bold, skillful and quick, it shouldn't matter if its presence is known."

"Perhaps. However, the law of survival has told the creature to move through the shadows in silence."

Yoshi spoke up tentatively. "Like Chelsea, I consider the tiger a menacing animal."

"Hm-m-m." Again the uncle smiled. "We see the animal differently. That is to be expected. Separate cultures, separate ideas. I have heard interesting stories about your country—some bad, some good." He chuckled as if all were funny. "While you are here, Tsuyoshi, I will try to see the world through your eyes, if you will try to see it though mine."

"Of course. I would like to learn more about Japanese ways."

The uncle nodded. "I'm glad. Now, let us go to the house, sit on the porch, admire the wisteria, drink beer and share our lives. My son, Shunsuke, has a fair command of English. He will join us as soon as he has finished in the barn." He stared at the pail. "Ah, I nearly forgot. My mother-in-law is waiting for the eels. She probably thinks I did not remember to buy them." Picking up the pail, he started for the door. "Come along Tsuyoshi."

Yoshi started after his uncle.

Chelsea wasn't sure if she was supposed to follow or not. She stood indecisively by a table.

At the door, Uncle Iiyama abruptly swung around, eyebrows raised high. "Ah, Miss Jarvis, please forgive me, I almost forgot you. My mother-in-law will be happy to serve you tea. Do you wish it brought out here or will you drink it in the house?"

Feeling her anger rise, Chelsea pressed her lips together. He was deliberately relegating her to the women's section.

Yoshi looked back and forth between Chelsea and Uncle Iiyama. In a quiet but determined voice he said, "I believe my friend would prefer a bottle of beer as we are having."

"Hm-m-m," said Uncle Iiyama, obviously annoyed.

Yoshi's voice was gentle but firm. "Uncle Iiyama, I don't mean to be disrespectful, I merely wish to point out that this is a difference between our two cultures."

Uncle Iiyama frowned.

An uneasy silence filled the room.

Then, from under the table Hiro burst out like a missile, his ray gun pointed first at Chelsea, then at Yoshi. "Za-a-p! Za-a-p!" he shouted. "*Shinda!*"

Midori rushed forward and yanked the ray gun from Hiro's hands. She pulled her son back behind the table and peeled off a string of Japanese words so fast Chelsea couldn't understand even one. Hiro wailed, tears pouring from his eyes. Ayako shrilled out a song, apparently in an effort to distract the child.

When the chaos subsided, Chelsea drew herself up in a dignified manner. With a smile to equal the uncle's, she said, "Iiyama-san, if you please, at this time, as Yoshi said, I would prefer a beer instead of tea. However, I don't want to interfere with you gentlemen conversing on the porch." She raised her chin. "If you wouldn't mind, I'd rather drink my beer beside the interesting rock spires and hot springs I noticed in your compound." She bowed.

Uncle Iiyama bowed back. "As you wish."

Yoshi grinned.

Chelsea felt as if she had successfully negotiated a difficult settlement. What's more, she thought, I did it without my hat.

CHAPTER 24

It was dusk, a gray light blurring the outlines of objects. Ayako and Midori locked up the warehouse and entered the home by a side shoji, herding the ray-gun-clutching boy with them.

The three men sat on the porch drinking beer. Now and then Midori slipped out through the front shoji with another bottle. She poured the liquid into the men's glasses and arranged the empty bottles beside the front steps.

Yoshi sat in a rattan chair near the wisteria-filled railing. He studied Chelsea's silhouette among the rocks that jutted up near the hot springs, her bag over one shoulder, beer bottle in her right hand. He examined the stoic faces of Uncle Iiyama and Shunsuke who sat in the rattan chairs to his right.

Earlier, he and Uncle Iiyama had compared life in academic and artistic worlds, moving on to discuss reasons for violent crimes in American cities. They considered pollution problems and finally skimmed across possible solutions for trade imbalances. Yoshi couldn't be certain of Uncle Iiyama's true feelings, although it seemed their views were not as far apart as he had assumed.

Shunsuke had showered in the outside stall by the hot springs, finishing just as Chelsea approached the rocks. Yoshi had heard him cry, *"Sumimasen,"* and saw him dash for the house, clad only in a brief towel. Not knowing whether to laugh or ignore the situation, he glanced at Uncle Iiyama for a cue. The uncle rolled his eyes so Yoshi did the same.

Now Shunsuke wore trousers and a kimono-like jacket. On his feet were dark blue, rubber-soled tabi called *"jikatabi."* Yoshi remembered reading about workmen using them. Prompted by his own mixed feelings of living with his parents, he asked Shunsuke, "Why do you stay here with your relatives?"

If he hadn't felt so relaxed by the beer, he wouldn't have made such a personal inquiry. He seldom pried into other people's lives.

"Wife's family three *cho-bu* own," Shunsuke replied laboriously. "Here!" He gestured widely to the surrounding land with his beer-glass hand, none of the liquid spilling.

Yoshi knew he was talking about the size of the land. He wondered about its equivalent in acreage but thought it best not to ask. The fellow was having enough trouble with English.

Shunsuke pointed to himself. "Me and Midori, we here after marry. Eight years ago. To help." He blinked as if not certain he could pull the words from his thoughts. "First, everybody rice farm. Very happy. Then Midori's father die." He took a deep breath and let the air out in a rush. "Her brother, Michio, lose eyes." He pointed to his own and his voice softened. "Michio go."

Yoshi noticed a tremor in Shunsuke's chin and felt it necessary to look away. When he glanced back, Shunsuke was drinking his beer.

Uncle Iiyama said, "Since Michio lost his eyesight, he lives at a shrine in the mountains." He nodded at the tall peaks to the north of the compound. "He seems more at peace up there."

In a steadier voice Shunsuke continued, "Midori's mother say, 'We no farm. Never again farm.' Many days she sit in room. Stare at tatami." He took another deep breath, letting the air out more slowly. "So, three years ago from Tokyo my mother and father come." He gestured with his glass at Uncle Iiyama. "They help us with new work. New life." Shunsuke waved his arms as a conductor might conclude a symphony and then he heaved a long sigh.

After a moment, Yoshi inquired gently, "Excuse me, but around here I noticed new rice plants and flooded fields. May I ask who does the farming now?"

"Other people," Shunsuke replied, looking at the mountains. "Others...."

Uncle Iiyama cleared his throat and said, "We hired a family to do the work. They live in a house on the main road." He stood up. "More beer, Tsuyoshi?"

Immediately, Midori appeared with a bottle in one hand and a small lit lantern in the other. She set the lantern down on the porch and looked at Yoshi questioningly.

He wondered if she had listened to their conversation. "No, thanks," he replied. "It's great beer, but I've had enough."

Uncle Iiyama nodded, waved Midori away and sat down again.

The landscape had faded, the sky nearly dark. Yoshi squinted at the odd-shaped rocks around the hot-springs, no longer able to see Chelsea. He surveyed the two men who sat beside him like soldiers, feet together, backs straight. He eyed the empty bottles on the porch, neatly arranged around the billed cap Chelsea had worn on the trip. It had fallen out of the fiber bag. On the way to the porch Uncle Iiyama had picked up the cap and placed it there.

Between the effect of alcohol and the approach of night, everything seemed more and more ethereal to Yoshi. He wondered if soon he might have nothing solid to walk on. So many questions he wanted to ask. Did Uncle Iiyama miss teaching at the university? Did Shunsuke miss working in the rice fields? What happened to Michio's eyes? Why hadn't he met Midori's mother?

But, even if he found a cautious way to ask these questions, he felt the answers would be vague. He sensed a hidden story here, a tragedy, something painful to Shunsuke. Maybe painful to them all. If he knew that story, he might decipher the inner feelings of these stiffly erect men who sat beside him.

Out of the darkness, Chelsea appeared, walking toward the house.

He wanted to race toward her and clasp her in his arms. Paralysis held him in his chair. Indecision. Fear. He would look like a fool. Too public a demonstration. He might fall down from too much beer; he had lost track of how much he had consumed.

Uncle Iiyama rose with the dignity of a retired general and called out, "Miss Jarvis, have you finished exploring?"

"If you have completed your conversation," she said as she reached the porch steps.

"We have." He waved at the sky. "Night creeps in on little cat's paws." With a chuckle, he peered at Yoshi as if to assess the effect of his poetic words.

Yoshi felt foolish but wasn't sure why.

"You may wish to bathe before dinner," the uncle said to him. "Your bedroom is the first on the left. There you will find a fresh yukata and slippers. Miss Jarvis, your room is next to Tsuyoshi's. The same items are available for you. There is only one tub." He issued a faint smile, removed his clogs, wiped his feet with a folded towel by the shoji and then entered the house.

Not until Chelsea came up on the porch, did Yoshi slip off his Italian loafers and brush his feet on the towel, symbolic, since his socks hadn't connected with oxcart contaminants. She removed her shoes and dropped them beside his.

Glancing behind him, Yoshi saw Shunsuke pick up the lantern and rearrange the bottles in a symmetrical manner, adding Chelsea's to the group, the three empty glasses in an outer row. Were these arrangements meaningful? An artistic expression? A propensity for an orderly life? He hoped he hadn't been expected to participate in the endeavor.

Uncle Iiyama's voice took on a commanding tone. "In our home we enjoy two living rooms." As if that needed further explanation, he slid back one of four shoji screens that divided the living room into two smaller rooms. Where they stood was carpeted, with a loveseat, two wooden chairs, a TV, lamps—all Western style . The other side of the shoji was tatami-floored and traditionally Japanese in appearance.

Uncle Iiyama took them to the other side of the entry hall and showed them the dining room, a chandelier in the shape of a miniature pagoda hanging above a teak table, four leather-cushioned chairs drawn up. "We eat dinner at eight," he announced.

They were not shown the kitchen or the five bedrooms, although Uncle Iiyama advised them of their existence and indicated where they were. The rooms were small but numerous, the house large, especially when Yoshi compared it to Great Uncle Nagata's two-room home in Odawara.

Even more amazing was the final room displayed by Uncle Iiyama. He called it his "Communication Base." Not only did it contain shelves packed with books but two high-tech computers, a laser printer and a fax machine. The room was closed off from the rest of the house by a heavy wooden door instead of a shoji.

All this, thought Yoshi, and yet Uncle Iiyama preferred an oxcart to a pickup truck for transporting large items? It was hard to fathom.

"I keep in touch," Uncle Iiyama said, waving both hands at his books and machines, "with clients, with the university and as much as possible with the world. Twice a year I go to Tokyo. I own a cubicle there, a two-tatami room, where I sleep on a futon and make tea on a hot plate. The rest of the time I make my contacts from here." He led them out of the room and closed the door.

Wearing flowered kimonos, Midori and Ayako served the four at the dining room table, Shunsuke still in his wrap-around jacket and trousers, Uncle Iiyama and the guests in yukatas, all in slippers. *"Itadakimasu,"* Uncle Iiyama said in the manner of a blessing.

Yoshi exchanged a look with Chelsea and opted for the chopsticks over the fork, also by his plate. Chelsea followed suit. He had heard that traditionally women ate separately from men. If so, was Chelsea's inclusion at the table because she was a guest?

Nothing was said during dinner. Yoshi was so intrigued with the food he didn't find the silence a problem. Instead of sake during the meal, beer was served, which surprised him. Following the sashimi came soup. Then a wide assortment of dishes, the fish broiled to perfection, the eels deliciously crunchy. Some tastes he didn't recognize, and he was too embarrassed to ask.

He wondered if it was common in this family for the women and little Toru to eat separately. And what about Midori's mother? Most likely she was in the kitchen. Would they never see her?

As he ate, Yoshi peripherally watched Chelsea. Her handling of the chopsticks was a bit awkward but not bad. She managed. Not every food was to her liking. The jellyfish remained untouched and she didn't eat all of her octopus. Near the end of the meal, while they ate *chazuke*, rice with fragrant tea poured over it, he met her eyes and she smiled warmly at him, sending a tingle down his spine.

After dinner Uncle Iiyama led them into the Western living room where Ayako served small cups of strong coffee, then bowed and left. Uncle Iiyama closed his eyes as if meditating. Shunsuke stared straight ahead. The complete silence in the room pressed in on Yoshi. At the dinner table, he had been too involved with examining the beauty of the food, enjoying the various tastes and smells and watching Chelsea to be bothered by the lack of conversation. Now, however, as he faced his two relatives without a table, minus a beer, with only a tiny cup of bitter coffee in his hands, the stillness seemed overwhelming.

Yoshi had no idea what to say. If somebody didn't start talking soon, he might have to excuse himself and escape to his room. He was afraid to look at Chelsea, who sat beside him. He was embarrassed to stare at Uncle Iiyama and uneasy to take another look at Shunsuke, who reminded him of a bomb ready to explode. Yoshi sat there, feeling like a dud, inspecting his coffee cup, adjusting his yukata, and wishing it were time to go to bed.

Just as he had given up hope, music drifted from the tatami-matted room on the other side of the closed shoji screens. The sounds of a koto and a drum and—he tried to identify the third instrument. A shamisen, that was it. The musicians must have entered the room through the shoji on the side porch.

Uncle Iiyama and Shunsuke rose in unison as if the sounds were a martial signal. Shunsuke slid aside the screen and Uncle Iiyama with a nod indicated Yoshi and Chelsea should enter the room.

For the first time since he had found himself in this alarming after-dinner predicament, Yoshi looked at Chelsea. He thought he detected nervousness in her half smile. Reaching out, he touched her fingers. They were like ice. Startled, he gave her hand a reassuring squeeze.

Always he had considered her in complete control of situations. Now she seemed as bothered as he was about being in this alien territory. They walked hand in hand toward the other room. He remembered the moments in the car after he had helped her escape from the airport. Then and now, the only times he had been aware she could be upset, her smooth surface ruffled. He had considered her fearless, cool, calculating, a goddess-like woman able to cope with all people and all situations. Now he realized that wasn't entirely so.

These thoughts brought him a sense of composure. At this point he felt he could handle his relatives, endure their periods of silence and deal with any embarrassments or misunderstandings he might have. Yes, he could adapt to the ways of his Japanese family and accept whatever any of them did or said. Perhaps this was because he knew that now he didn't have to deal with these problems alone. Chelsea was with him.

CHAPTER 25

Midori and Ayako, playing stringed instruments, and another woman, playing a small drum, knelt on pillows at one end of the tatami-matted room. Chelsea noticed Uncle Iiyama's piercing look and let go of Yoshi's hand, thinking it might not be the proper way to act. Carefully she knelt on a pillow by the low table opposite the musicians. Shunsuke entered last and closed the shoji behind him.

Why did her heart race this way? Chelsea wondered. Nobody here was going to hurt her. Neither the yakuza nor the government security guys knew where she was. This wasn't a courtroom. No trial, no client, no opponent. Not important what these people thought about her. Or was it?

She realized something different was going on here. This wasn't a win-lose situation. Yet how she acted seemed important, increasingly so since the first night she had shared dinner with Yoshi. She wanted him to be proud of her; it was a long time since anyone's opinion had been this important. She bit her lower lip, looked around and listened to the music, determined not to consider her relationships any more.

Behind the three musicians, attached to the wall, was a dull gold, three-sectional screen, painted on it a forest scene. Uncle Iiyama's work? Perhaps, for in the shadows crouched a tiger.

At first glance, the three women who knelt in front of the screen reminded Chelsea of a woodcut print, something the Japanese artist Utamaro might have created. On closer scrutiny, she realized no *ukiyo-e* print-maker would have wanted to portray the old woman who played the drum. Her hair, smoke gray, was cropped short, hacked off unevenly in an unbecoming style that looked self-inflicted. She wore a coarse cotton kimono of charcoal black that cast a gray pallor on her skin. Her eyes were haunted, as if she saw an inner terror. Chelsea couldn't stop looking at her, so different from the other two women, who wore brightly flowered silk kimonos, their long hair hanging down in back like dark waterfalls—Midori's exceptionally shiny, Ayako's a white streak cresting her head and cascading down.

The instrument Midori plucked was similar to a banjo although the sound more resonant. Ayako played a kind of harp that lay flat on the floor. The two women, their faces serene, produced notes of elegant dissonance, their fingers moving over the strings with extraordinary grace.

The gray-haired woman beat the small drum with robot precision.

It was cooler than in the other living room. Chelsea imagined how in wintertime the hearth in the center would be uncovered and a fire lit. Where would the smoke go? Disbursed in the thatch above? Or filling up the room, hazy and gray like the old woman?

On the low table was a tray with china cups the size of large thimbles, a porcelain container shaped like a bud vase and a bowl of water. As Uncle Iiyama poured liquid from the porcelain container into three of the cups, Chelsea smelled a sweet aroma. *Sake,* she supposed, remembering when she and Yoshi had shared the drink at the inn.

Midori began to sing on that same strange scale played by the instruments. Not the kind of music Chelsea knew, yet what she might want to hear more often, soft, tender notes that evoked pictures of silks and spices.

Uncle Iiyama set the filled cups in front of Yoshi, Chelsea and Shunsuke and an empty cup in front of himself. He stared at his cup and stroked his mustache.

Yoshi leaned forward, picked up the porcelain container and poured liquid into Uncle Iiyama's cup. The hint of a smile crossed the uncle's face. He nodded his appreciation, picked up his cup, and consumed its contents in one swallow.

In a ritualistic manner, Shunsuke and Yoshi picked up their cups, both holding them in the same manner and drank. When Chelsea tried to imitate, her hand trembled slightly. She steadied it. The liquor felt warm and pleasantly fiery as it went down her throat. It tasted different from *sake*. Stronger. Much stronger.

Yoshi dipped his empty cup into the water bowl, then poured in more of the fiery liquid and set his cup before Uncle Iiyama, who immediately drained it and rinsed the cup in the water. With a bow of his head, Uncle Iiyama returned the empty cup to Yoshi and refilled it for him. A ritual, Chelsea realized. And Yoshi had surprised the uncle with his knowledge of it.

Her cup was full again. She drank it and felt giddy, what with all the beer before and during dinner and now this wild stuff.

The music ceased. Midori demurely crossed to the other end of the room, opened a reddish-wood cabinet with brass corners and took out a lacquer tray that held four damp towels. She distributed the towels, returned the lacquer tray to the cabinet, and while the four cleansed their hands and blotted their lips, gathered the drinking cups onto the container tray. Finally, after collecting the four towels, Midori bowed and carried the tray from the room.

Uncle Iiyama waited until the screen closed before rising and walking to the cabinet with measured steps.

Another family ritual, thought Chelsea. Did it make them feel more like a family? Draw them closer together?

He returned to the table with two bottles and four glasses on a brass tray.

Chelsea's eyes widened. Whiskey and soda? If she drank that on top of the beer and the fiery stuff, she might cease to function or worse get sick. Glancing sideways at Yoshi, she noticed his face had a pink hue.

Once again there was silence. The uncle, his eyes closed, knelt statue like on his pillow. Chelsea wondered if he was waiting for a signal. Shunsuke, his palms resting on his thighs, stared straight ahead as if in a trance. She readjusted her knees. The room felt hot.

Midori returned. The music began as before, moving into a song. Uncle Iiyama opened his eyes and poured whiskey and soda into three glasses. In the fourth he added less whiskey and more soda. To Chelsea's relief, he placed the weaker drink before her, amusement in his eyes.

Shortly after they started drinking the whiskey, Uncle Iiyama asked Chelsea politely, "Would you mind describing your work and how it relates to Japan?"

Because she felt relaxed and was glad Uncle Iiyama spoke to her with apparent interest, she eagerly portrayed her life as a lawyer, interpreted the spokes in the litigation wheel, jabbered about how her mission was to help people solve problems legally, ones they couldn't handle personally. She moved on to her reason for coming to Japan: to negotiate a contract for a...a friend. Her throat dried up. She stopped talking. She felt she had babbled on too long. Besides, her thoughts were getting hazy.

Yoshi started talking in what Chelsea thought was a surprisingly animated fashion. He explained how Chelsea became the carrier of lurid photographs obviously taken for blackmail purposes. How he had met Chelsea and all of the difficulties that had happened to her, described Kagawa and the man in dark glasses who had strong-armed him at the noodle stand, recounted Grandmother's clever rescue at the airport. "We are hiding from the owners of the photographs," Yoshi proclaimed. "I believe it is a yakuza syndicate."

At the word "yakuza" the women ceased playing. Midori and Ayako rose quickly and knelt at the end of the table, concern on their faces. The gray woman remained by the painted screen and stared at her drum as if it might tell her something.

"Also," Yoshi concluded, waving his glass dramatically, "we may be hiding from Japanese security agents who might be affiliated with the yakuza."

Uncle Iiyama, his mouth turned down thoughtfully, seemed to be digesting the information. After a few moments, he said, "Best to stay hidden until we can plan your escape." He exchanged a knowing look with Shunsuke who nodded.

While Shunsuke translated Yoshi's information to Ayako and Midori, Uncle Iiyama poured another drink for the three men. When he reached for Chelsea's glass, she giggled and shook her head. To her horror, she realized she was sitting cross-legged, the hem of her yukata bunched up at her knees. With a squeal of dismay, she scrambled into a kneeling position and bowed low to Uncle Iiyama, her hands prayer-like. "Sorry, sorry."

This brought an explosion of hilarity, even from Yoshi, whose face Chelsea thought was turning into the color of rose petals. She giggled some more.

For some reason, Yoshi began to clap with a staccato rhythm.

Chelsea clapped along with him.

Everybody clapped,

Uncle Iiyama started to pour another round, but Yoshi turned his glass upside down, the last vestiges of his whiskey spreading across the table. Yoshi tried to blot it away with the sleeve of his yukata, causing another round of laughter. Midori hurried over, shaking her hands as if not to worry. Kneeling beside him, she set his glass back on the tray and used a handkerchief pulled from the sleeve of her kimono to quickly mop up the remaining drops, all the while making little hushing sounds to him.

"*Arigato*," he said to her.

"*Do itashimashite*," she replied, head lowered.

Abruptly, Uncle Iiyama brandished his arms through the air as if involved in a sword fight. "Nobody shall stop us from moon-viewing," he cried and rose to his feet like a drunken warrior.

Shunsuke translated Uncle Iiyama's English to Midori and Ayako who applauded.

Chelsea tried to rise but fell against Yoshi, who was also having difficulty standing. They clung to each other, laughing, and barely managed not to fall backwards onto the table. At last they gained their feet and staggered out of the tatami-floored room, following Uncle Iiyama. Shunsuke came after them. Midori and Ayako brought up the rear.

In the middle of the Western carpet, Chelsea stopped, holding onto the back of the loveseat for support. "Why doesn't the gray lady come with us?" she cried, waving back at the tatami room.

Uncle Iiyama threw open the front door and stood there as if ready to defend his house against an enemy invasion. "That is Midori's mother," he announced without looking back at Chelsea. "She is a *mibojin*."

Chelsea wavered toward him. "What's that mean?"

"A widow. The person left. The one who has not yet died."

"I don't get it."

He turned around and looked at Chelsea. "Physically she is alive; spiritually she is dead."

Chelsea blinked and tried to concentrate on the meaning of his words. "How sad!"

"*Hai. hai.* We cannot seem to help her. Even her brother, who heads a large Tokyo corporation, tried to help her. She told him to go away." He smiled wryly, his body swaying like bamboo in the wind. "You see, Miss Jarvis, in our isolated countryside, we feel we must solve our own problems." He faced outside again and reeled forward, shouting, "Where is the moon? Show your face, oh wondrous moon."

Yoshi staggered onto the porch after him, his arms open like an orator. He declaimed,

"In the ocean of the sky,
Borne on rising waves of cloud,
The moon ship goes a-gliding by
Through a forest of stars."

"Ah, so!" cried Uncle Iiyama. He jammed his feet into his clogs and clumped down the steps. "Do you hear that, spirit of the waters?" he cried toward the hot springs. "Our Tsuyoshi Moore quotes Hitomaro. He must be Japanese."

"I **am** Japanese," Yoshi announced. "I am a two-culture man."

"*Banzai!*" shouted Shunsuke with obvious approval. He raced down the steps. Uncle Iiyama and Yoshi charged after him.

It was dark outside. Chelsea heard the three men singing someplace near the hot springs. She paused on the porch, blinking, Midori and Ayako behind her. As she started down the steps, she stumbled and the ladies caught her.

"I'm drunk," she muttered. "Not as drunk as those guys. Still, I better watch out. Don't want to fall into the hot springs. I might not even feel the heat."

CHAPTER 26

The house glowed like a giant lantern, illuminating the scene some twenty feet around it. Chelsea leaned forward, trying to see where the three men had gone. She could hear them laughing and talking in Japanese but couldn't see them. Ah, there they were, Yoshi's arms outstretched. She smiled and imagined him still spouting poetry. The men danced in front of the steaming pool, the monster rocks, lit from below, towering over them like primeval guards.

    She drifted along the cedar bark path, not feeling much of anything, not knowing if the air was hot or cold, not aware of where she was. Behind her, Midori and Ayako giggled from the porch. They called to her in Japanese. Something about being careful? Of what? The world looked magical. To her befuddled brain, nothing else mattered. Stars crowded the sky. Billions of stars. No, not stars. Bright souls in a vast, black amphitheater. Spirits gathered to watch over people on earth. Around her, supernatural creatures began to rise up like genies. She bowed and bid them all welcome. Then she noticed the bare outlines of twisted trees beyond the rocks at the entrance to the compound. They looked like Numpkins.

Numpkins. The name rushed in like a breeze from childhood. One Christmas, Aunt Laura gave her a book about the deformed creatures that lived in an otherwise beautiful world. She read and reread the book, cried over it, until the pages were old and tattered, until one day her mother threw the book away along with a bin of empty whiskey bottles. Yes, the trees along the road looked like poor, pathetic Numpkins.

Why am I here? she wondered. She turned in a slow circle, searching for a clue. Spreading her arms out sideways like wings, she faced the mountains that rose in abrupt silhouettes. Her body felt on automatic pilot. She stared above the peaks and waited for her descent to the runway. At any moment landing lights would appear, up there where the sky wasn't as dark and fewer souls twinkled. "I'm not so tipsy that I can't wait for the lights," she muttered, squinting, trying to understand what she looked at and why. Then she noticed a huge light inching up behind the mountain.

She made the connection. "Enter, great moon," she cried. "Welcome to the Tigers' House."

A man's voice beside her said softly, "You're the most beautiful woman I've ever known."

She drew in a quick breath. Yoshi. Here. Beside her. Standing on the cedar bark path. He had left the men at the pool and come back for her. A current of pleasure spread through her body.

"I welcome you and the moon," she said and held her arms out to him.

He gathered her in. "You're more enchanting than the wondrous moon."

"Me enchanting? No, no." With a titter, she leaned her head against his chest. "I am plain old Chelsea, prowling around, hunting through the dark night to capture sweet, sweet Yoshi."

"Chelsea." He breathed her name as if it were a magic spell, then kissed her hair, her neck, and her lips, more and more eagerly, like a young lover experiencing passion for the first time.

So intensely did she respond that she thought her body had melted, her legs giving away. "Oh-h-h," she murmured and sank into a feather world.

He staggered under her weight.

They collapsed in a heap, still clinging to each other as if to let go might be the end of them both. Their fall to the path didn't seem unusual, rather a natural progression down together to a mystic bed of cedar bark and pine needles. It seemed of no consequence that Midori and Ayako stood on the porch giggling. Nor that Uncle Iiyama and Shunsuke danced and sang by the hot springs. All that was important was Chelsea and Yoshi intertwined.

But then he let go of her and sat up. "Good grief, I'm going to be sick."

"No! No!" she cried, not feeling well herself. "Not now."

"Sorry." He stumbled to his feet and lurched off into the darkness.

She heard him retch, a cross between bones crunching and a distraught chicken cackling.

In an attempt to clear her mind, she sat up and pinched her cheeks. That didn't help. She peered around. Uncle Iiyama and Shunsuke still cavorted by the hot springs. Midori and Ayako had gone inside. Again she heard Yoshi throw up and pressed her hands against her lips to keep from gagging herself. She wanted to help him. But how? She couldn't help anybody when she felt so blotto.

The full moon illuminated the landscape with the eerie look of blue neon. Long shadows stood behind the towering rocks and the Numpkin trees. Wisteria blossoms on the porch railing shone like glass beads.

Struggling to her feet, Chelsea tried valiantly not to fall down again but her legs seemed made of putty. "Yoshi," she called as she crawled down the cedar bark path, "are you okay?"

"No," he wailed.

She found him behind the outdoor shower and managed to make it to her feet, this time staying upright. There must be something she could do for him. She blinked at the shower stall. "Cold water," she cried. "Might help you. Might help us both."

Yoshi, on his knees, was bent over the empty fish pail. The combined smell made her gag. "Are you done yet?" she whimpered.

"For now," he replied with a sigh that was a partial moan.

"Then move over," she urged.

"Jesus," he said and patted her back while she threw up in the pail.

****

Daylight. Head throbbing, mouth like an outhouse, body sore all over, awful memories flooding in. Chelsea groaned and pulled the cover over her eyes—God, how they ached! Apparently she hadn't been completely drunk or she wouldn't remember so much. She burrowed deeper under the cover, trying to turn off her mind, unable to escape the painful pictures of last night's antics—the whole embarrassing scene imprinted on her mind never to be forgotten.

After throwing up in the fish pail, she had felt a little better although more dizzy and disoriented. She had suggested the shower and he had readily agreed.

At that point, she flung off her yukata and shoes. He did the same. They crowded into the outdoor closet-sized cubicle, no curtain on the open side. In retrospect, she couldn't imagine how she had so easily removed her clothes and tossed them aside. At the time, to strip naked seemed the normal thing to do. Naked, the only way to be. And he had done the same with equal abandon.

What surprised both of them, however, was the shower. Or rather that the levered faucet was in the middle of the wall, waist high rather than above the head, and no indication which way to shove it for hot or cold. A long-handled wooden bucket, a wooden ladle, a large cake of soap and a sponge rested under the faucet. Also in the stall was a three-legged stool.

Yoshi inspected the faucet as if it were a complex machine. He lifted the lever. Boiling water shot out. They screeched and jumped around. He slammed the lever down, repositioned it and carefully lifted it up again. Cold water poured forth. They roared with laughter and splashed each other. She filled the bucket and dumped water over his head. He grabbed the bucket, filled it, and threw water in her face. They squealed and howled and hopped about.

At one point Chelsea stood on the stool. "I'm the great tiger queen," she shouted. "Oops." She fell and he caught her, both of them giggling like children. Then he stood on the stool, swaying. "Behold the King of the Night," he shouted. With a yelp, he slipped off and she clutched him. They laughed so hard they collapsed in a heap. They took more turns, each time falling off with gales of laughter until Yoshi fell against the side of the stall and it rocked like a boat. They shrieked with terror and sank to the floor hugging each other in desperation. "Titanic going down," yelled Yoshi.

Less active after that, she scrubbed his back with the sponge. He scrubbed hers. They ladled water on their faces and started to sing, "Show Me the Way to Go Home," forgot the words after the second line and switched to "I'm Just a Poor Wayfaring Stranger," which Yoshi belted out while she played an imaginary horn, tooting to the sky.

How long Midori and Ayako stood outside the shower with the towels, Chelsea had no idea. But when Yoshi saw them, he quickly pressed the water lever down, bowed formally, and babbled something in Japanese. All she could think of to say was *"Moshi, Moshi,"* which she thought meant hello. In retrospect this morning it was a dumb thing to say because those words were usually used to answer the telephone.

The two Japanese ladies gently dried off the two Americans, recovered their *yukatas* and shoes, assisted them in dressing, and helped them toward the house. Chelsea, while on the porch fumbling for her indoor slippers, heard Uncle Iiyama yell for them to stay outside and join him for a soak in the hot springs.

Ayako shook her head and shouted something back in a surprisingly sharp tone. With Midori's help, she propelled her guests through the front doorway, down the hall, and into their respective bedrooms, murmuring encouragement all the way.

Chelsea didn't remember lying down. Perhaps she was asleep before she reached her futon, automatic pilot again kicking in.

Now, as daylight filtered through the shoji, her head was a drum, a devil beating on it, and her stomach was full of grasshoppers. The thought of facing anyone who might have seen her last night was humiliating. She suppressed a groan, not wanting to advertise her condition through the walls. How did Yoshi feel this morning? Probably worse for he'd consumed more alcohol.

What must he think of her? What must his relatives think? She had wanted to make Yoshi proud. Instead, she had given the performance of a wanton creature, rolling with him on the cedar bark, urping in the fish pail, leaping about naked, caterwauling in the shower. God almighty, it couldn't have been worse.

She sat up. It does no good to linger over past regrets she kept telling herself, although she didn't believe it. Swallowing hard, she decided she had to pull herself together and handle today's problems. Perhaps Yoshi wouldn't remember about last night. She doubted it. Probably he would be as embarrassed about their moonlight caper as she. Oh, Lord, what a dreadful episode.

Quietly she rose, retied the belt on her yukata, and rubbed her temples. Sliding open the shoji to the hall, she listened. Not a sound. Good. She tiptoed down the hall to the bathroom.

A few moments after she returned to her room, while she was digging in the fiber bag for her bottle of aspirin, she heard a soft knock at her hall shoji.

She froze. "Yes?"

"*Shitsurei, shimasu.*"

The voice was low and husky, not one she recognized. Chelsea slid back the screen. There, head bowed, knelt the gray woman in the black kimono. Beside her was a lacquer tray that held a teapot, cup, small bowl of rice crackers and three squares of dry seaweed that looked more like pieces of carbon.

"*Do mo arigato,*" Chelsea said.

The old woman tapped the teapot. "*Habucha.*" She rubbed her stomach and patted her temples, squeezing her face as if in pain. Again she tapped the pot.

Chelsea nodded and gladly took the tray. The old woman's pantomime had indicated the tea would make her feel better. After an exchange of bows, the woman closed the shoji and left Chelsea with the notion that a ghost had made a brief appearance.

Carefully removing the teapot lid, Chelsea sniffed. The contents had a musty odor. A close examination of the pot's interior revealed no big tea leaves, instead tiny dark bits of something or other. She decided to chance it.

Her first sips were tentative. A bland flavor, like she imagined roasted rice might taste. Maybe an herb tea. Nice in a way. Settling. More sips. The liquid felt soothing on her throat. She swallowed two aspirin with a second cup and ate a cracker, the snapping sound sending needles through her head. A third cup. Feeling slightly better, although no less embarrassed, she crawled back onto her futon and drifted off to sleep.

Later a sharp rap on the hall shoji woke her up. Uncle Iiyama's voice, loud, tense, called, "Miss Jarvis."

"Yes?"

"Imperative that you dress immediately and come to the porch. Bring your bag."

"Why?"

"I have received a disturbing message from our field caretaker."

"What's wrong?"

"He said he met a man from the yakuza who is looking for you."

Chelsea bolted to her feet.

"Hurry," said Uncle Iiyama. "You and Yoshi must leave the house at once."

CHAPTER 27

Yoshi staggered through the front doorway, his mind in a fog. His shirt wasn't buttoned and his belt was a snake needing to be tamed. Why were his shoes on the porch? He peered at them, lined up with others. Beside his shoes, a cap—Chelsea's.

She stood on the porch in front of him muttering, "Don't see anybody, do you? How much time've we got? How'd they find us? What's happening?" Her questions sounded garbled. She crunched on a piece of dried seaweed brought from her breakfast tray.

Yoshi's insides gurgled at the sound of her eating. He swallowed hard. He'd only been able to drink half a cup of tea, his stomach jumping around, and his head full of cactus spines. Now he wished for the sheets of seaweed and bowl of rice crackers he vaguely remembered seeing on his tray.

I'm on the front porch for a reason, he informed himself, blinking. He fumbled with the buttons on his shirt, managing to secure two in their holes. He got his belt buckle fastened.

Then he remembered the knock on his screen. He looked up. Uncle Iiyama stood below the porch, a pack on his back, a walking stick in one hand. Yoshi's eyes widened. Instantly his mind cleared. Yakuza coming! Good grief!

Uncle Iiyama said, "Your belongings, are they ready to go?"

"Yes," answered Chelsea. She indicated the fiber bag beside her.

Yoshi gulped. "I'm all packed," he cried and rushed back into the house.

Ayako came down the hall, pulling his suitcase.

Do mo arigato, Yoshi stammered with a bow. He grabbed the case and lurched out onto the porch.

Uncle Iiyama glared at him. "Put on your shoes."

"Yes, yes, of course." As he jammed his feet into them, he noticed Chelsea's were gone.

They followed Uncle Iiyama to the north side of the warehouse and plunged into an area of heavy brush, sweeping aside branches and bushes as they moved forward. Behind a large spruce tree, a narrow path led through a wooded area and wound up the mountainside. Uncle Iiyama, his back as straight as his staff, strode on without pausing. They stumbled after him, Yoshi having trouble dragging his suitcase, Chelsea continually looking behind.

After a little more than an hour, they reached a level bend in the trail. To one side, a fallen tree had been fashioned into a bench. Uncle Iiyama stopped. "For now we are safe," he said. "You cannot be seen from here. Relax. Ahead the climb is more difficult."

Chelsea collapsed onto the bench. "Not used to this," she muttered with a furtive look down the trail. She crammed the rest of the *nori* into her mouth as if that would make her available for anything.

Yoshi tried to hide the effect her eating had on his stomach by performing four knee bends. He glanced at his watch, dumbfounded to find it almost noon. How could he have slept so long? At home he was always up by six, at the gym by seven. Good grief!

He stared up at the mountainside. "Where are we going?" he asked Uncle Iiyama.

"To *Oinarisan,* a small shrine. Few people know of its existence.

"Is that where Midori's brother lives?"

"Yes. Michio is there by himself."

"A shame for a blind man to be alone."

Uncle Iiyama looked away.

Yoshi wished for the words back.

With one hand Uncle Iiyama smoothed the sides of his moustache, integrating the hairs with his beard. "To live by himself is Michio's desire," he said finally. "Not only is he blind, he is also disfigured, injured in an automobile accident. The vehicle exploded and his father died in the fire. Since Michio was the driver; he felt responsible." Uncle Iiyama raised his staff in a nothing-I-can-do gesture. "Although his physical wounds have healed, his mental wounds have not."

"Sorry," was all Yoshi could think of to say.

Uncle Iiyama cleared his throat "As for matters at hand, I was told this morning that someone in the Matsue area is looking for you both—the man who took Miss Jarvis to the airport."

"Kagawa," Chelsea and Yoshi said together.

"*Hai.* Yesterday afternoon this man charged into my uncle's house in Odawara."

Yoshi caught his breath. Thinking Chelsea might have lost tract of the connection, he said, "That's Great Uncle Nagata's house."

"I know," she replied.

He winced. Of course. She'd keep track of people no matter how tired she was and she looked exhausted. Dark circles pooled under her eyes and her shoulders slumped. Straightening his back, he shoved aside his weariness. If Chelsea needed physical help, he would be ready.

Chelsea said to Uncle Iiyama, "How did Kagawa find us?"

"He figured it was Tsuyoshi who spirited you from the airport. When he arrived at Uncle Nagata's house, he informed his daughter-in-law—the only person there at the time— that through his database he had located all of Tsuyoshi's relatives in Japan. He was certain Miss Jarvis had taken refuge with one of them. 'I shall visit each family member until I find Miss Jarvis,' he informed Kayako. 'Your house is closest and first on my list.' He carefully examined the living room and bedroom, looking under any possible hiding space. Then, apologizing for the disturbance, he bowed and left.

Yoshi leaned forward. " I have cousins near Odawara. Did he visit them next?"

"No. Kayako phoned my mother to warn her. Mr. Kagawa must have traced her call because several hours later he appeared in Kyoto at mother's gate. He said he must find Miss Jarvis before his boss discovered she was missing and before something catastrophic happened to her. He insisted his only concern was for the safety of Miss Jarvis because other people—I'll use his words—*are out to get her*. He went on to say, 'I have a deal for her to consider if she wishes to remain alive.'"

Chelsea shivered and glanced down the path.

Yoshi squeezed her arm to show his support.

"It seems," said Uncle Iiyama, "that not only the yakuza wishes to recover your envelope,"

"I considered destroying it." Chelsea said. "but thought either they wouldn't believe me or they'd seek revenge for my doing it." She bit her lower lip. "What's this 'deal' Kagawa offers?"

"Your safe exit from Japan and $20,000 transferred into your bank account after you deliver the envelope as instructed."

Chelsea shook her head. "I won't do it."

Uncle Iiyama raised his eyebrows. "Mother told me you would say that. She called Mr. Kagawa *machi no shirami*—lice of the town."

"A good description," said Yoshi. He sat down beside Chelsea, hoping to allay her fears. To Uncle Iiyama he said, "Did Kagawa recognize Grandmother from the airport?"

"He did and congratulated her on her cleverness in spilling her basket there. He said he regretted the injury to her hand from the broken glass. Mother displayed her undamaged hands and told him he was mistaken. Some other elderly lady must have caused his airport difficulties. When he grew angry, she suggested he walk with her in the garden so he could regain his calm and not let life confuse him. After the walk, she served him tea."

Yoshi smiled. "Grandmother would serve tea to the devil with the same unflappable dignity." He noticed Chelsea still staring down the trail. Occasionally he, too, gave it a glance. Swallowing hard and attempting to remain composed, he said to Uncle Iiyama, "How did you find out about all of this?"

"This morning Mother took her usual walk to the fish market. Thinking she might be followed, she ducked inside a stall, borrowed a vendor's phone and called me. That was three hours ago. When I woke you up, I had just received another phone call. From the people who tend our rice paddies. They said a black limousine stopped near the field where they were working. A tough-looking man with tattoos on his neck opened the window and asked them where the tiger-maker lived. They said they didn't know."

Uncle Iiyama took off his pack and set it on the bench. From a side pocket he removed a pair of binoculars. "Eventually this man will find our compound. He may already have. Wait here while I have a look." Like a tiger preparing to size up its prey, he crept to an overhanging ledge, stretched out on his stomach and peered below.

The temperature was mild, thin clouds scattered across the sky. The fragrant smell of the forest reminded Yoshi of his mother's perfume. It was hard to comprehend the need to run away, that this situation was serious. Should he be afraid? Uncle Iiyama had said they were safe for now.

Wanting to relax Chelsea, who kept looking back at the path, he ventured, "How do you feel?"

"Improving. How about you?"

"Better than a while ago." His stomach growled. "Excuse me," he murmured. Another gurgle, an even louder one.

"Here, saved these from my tray." She dug into her slack's pocket and gave him a handful of rice crackers. They might help.

"Thanks." He tossed the crackers into his mouth and started to chew. Abruptly he stopped.

Chelsea jumped up. "What's the matter?"

For a moment he froze, listening. "Someone," he sputtered, pointing down the trail. Unable to say any more he indicated she should hide behind the bench.

He slipped into the bushes that fringed the path, his mouth full of crackers, his heart pounding. Eyes focused on the path, he stole around the side of a large rock. Now he heard the rustling of leaves. Whoever it was must be just beyond the cedar trees. He didn't dare chew. Even his breathing was too loud. The crackers were dissolving but if he swallowed, he might choke. Take it easy, he told himself. Cautiously he slipped forward.

Then he saw them—two deer, browsing on leaves. They looked up, sniffed the air, saw him and crashed off into the underbrush.

He chewed up the rest of the crackers, swallowed hard and returned up the trail. "No need to hide," he said with a little laugh. "I should've realized it was only animals. We're safe up here."

"Maybe so," she said, "but in my mind I keep seeing an apparition of Kagawa. How can you be so calm in this situation?"

"I'm glad I appear calm." He fastened the last button on his shirt and shot a look down the trail.

Uncle Iiyama returned and announced, "In front of our house is a limousine."

The full danger struck Yoshi like icy needles.

Uncle Iiyama stroked his beard. "I shall hurry back and slip unseen into the warehouse to work on my bronze tiger. The *lice of the town* must not suspect where I have been." He looked from Yoshi to Chelsea as if judging their capabilities. "This path leads to the shrine. When you arrive, Tsuyoshi, ring the bell, bow and clap your hands. Hopefully, you know the proper way to do it. When Michio appears, explain why you have come. You must speak in Japanese as Michio speaks no English."

"What about the bell?" asked Yoshi. "Won't Kagawa hear it and know where we are?"

"I doubt if its sound would travel. The shrine is in a grove of trees and among boulders. Anyway, the only path up is well hidden. Without it, climbing equipment would be needed."

Uncle Iiyama reached into his pack, brought out a cloth-wrapped package and set it in Chelsea's bag. "In this *furoshiki* is your meal fixed by Michio's mother. She walks to the shrine twice a week to deliver food. Tomorrow is her day, so she will bring more for you then."

"How long should we stay up there?" Chelsea asked.

"Depends on the situation. Shunsuke or I will come up to let you know." After pocketing his binoculars, he slipped his pack back on. "Under no circumstances should you use your cell phone," he added.

For a few seconds the three stood there looking at each other as if further words were needed. None came, so they all bowed.

Then Uncle Iiyama strode down the trail, his back as straight as his walking stick.

CHAPTER 28

At first the upward path was easy, a gentle zigzag that leveled off to a sweet-smelling cedar forest. Unseen, a nightingale sang as if its life depended upon how well it performed. The forest thinned to dwarfed conifers. The trail steepened, precariously narrow in places, footing rocky and slippery, a ravine on one side, a rock wall on the other. Yoshi longed for tennis shoes. Italian loafers had no place on a mountainside.

The path grew even more treacherous. He noted Chelsea ahead, leaning in against the wall or clutching at whatever might give her stability—limbs of trees that rose from the chasm to edge the trail. In one instance, she grabbed a bush that gave away. In time, he leaned forward to steady her. Later, after he too slipped, he pushed down the handle of his suitcase and used it like a cane, edging upward sideways.

It took over two hours to reach their destination. They came upon it suddenly, after the trail passed between two massive boulders, in a pocket of tall pine trees, hidden from below by a dip in the terrain. The torii was an impressive gateway, not so much because of its height, around eight feet, as for its color, brilliant vermillion that looked freshly painted; a thick rope looped down from its lower crossbar. A precisely laid stone path led through the torii to the steps of a small, equally bright vermillion building partially built into the rocky cliff. The wooden structure had a steeply pitched roof, thatched and curved upward at the eaves. At the foot of the steps was a post. From the top a bell angled out and a long rope hung down..

On a pedestal nearby stood an ancient stone statue of an animal on its haunches. Yoshi had read that it was usual for a fox, a *kitsune*, to be erected before a shrine to Inari, the spirit of cereals and farm products. The well-swept grounds that surrounded the shrine branched out from the tori several feet and then back to the cliff, the entire area swept clean and enclosed with a low, wooden fence.

At the bottom of the shrine steps, Yoshi rang the bell, bowed twice and then sharply clapped his hands two times, actions he knew were necessary to get the attention of the spirit Inari and ward off evil spirits. Holding his hands prayerfully, he bowed deeply to express his respect for the good spirit.

He heard a male voice behind him and realized that someone other than Chelsea was there. Startled, he turned.

It was Michio. Thick, pinkish scars on his cheeks had pulled his eye sockets down so that only white showed for his eyes. His lips were drawn into a crooked smile. Yoshi didn't want to stare at this disfigured, sightless man, who stood there in a black kimono and straw sandals, leaning on a cane. Yet he found it difficult to look away from him, for the pink scars stood out like signals. Michio's hair, soot black and neatly-combed, reached his shoulders and a few black whiskers jutted from his chin. The skin on his arms and neck was a weathered brown.

"*Donata desu ka?*" Michio asked softly, questioning who the intruders were.

"*Watashi no ojisan Iiyama desu,*" replied Yoshi, explaining about his family relationship. "*To watashi no-tomadachi,*" he added, wanting Michio to know his friend was also here. "*Tsuyoshi to Chelsea,*" he concluded.

"Hi," said Chelsea. "I mean *konnichi wa.*"

Michio bowed.

Instinctively, Yoshi bowed back.

In halting Japanese, Yoshi told Michio that he and Chelsea had come to the shrine for protection and didn't know how long they might have to stay.

Michio listened attentively, then waved his cane for them to follow him.

To the left of the shrine enclosure, hollowed from the cliff, was a cave, its narrow opening hidden behind a large boulder. Michio said it was his home. He indicated the futon inside the cave entrance was an extra one his mother sometimes used. He hoped it would not be a problem to share it.

Chelsea and Yoshi exchanged furtive looks.

In spare words Michio expressed the importance of caring for *O-Inari-san*, that everything must be kept clean and orderly. When Yoshi asked him who had painted the shrine and the torii, Michio answered by displaying his hands.

"*So des'ka?*" Yoshi said, amazed.

Michio straightened his back and nodded.

Quickly Yoshi told him he had done a professional job on everything. Then he attempted a long explanation about what had happened the last five days and how concerned he was for Chelsea's welfare. He tried hard to speak correctly. But he didn't know the dialect in this part of Japan and realized he sounded stilted and often used wrong words. However, Michio seemed to understand what he said for he nodded frequently.

Yoshi was glad to communicate in Japanese but the labor of it made him sweat, even as a cold wind blew and Chelsea shivered. She put on her sweater. His sweater, he remembered with pleasure. He wiped his brow on his shirt sleeve and slipped his other arm protectively around her.

Michio gestured for them to enter his cave. It was dim inside, the only light from the portable charcoal stove on which a brass teakettle gently steamed. As Michio prepared tea, Yoshi unrolled the futon—a thin mat with a comforter-like blanket. Mentally he measured the size and decided it could fit over two people if they huddled together. It would be difficult to nestle with Chelsea and remain a gentleman, but he was determined not to impose himself upon her. Besides, even if by some chance a mutual feeling developed, the cave was not a private place. Although Michio could not see, surely he would know.

Yoshi caught her eyes on him, a half smile on her face. What was she thinking? How did she feel about him? Had his drunken antics last night destroyed any chance he might have? He smiled back, feeling foolish, juvenile. He didn't know what to do or say.

Michio brought them a cup of steaming tea, apologizing that he only had one extra cup but that perhaps they could sip from separate sides.

Yoshi said they appreciated his generosity.

Chelsea knelt on the futon. "Hey, come on," she said to Yoshi, "kneel down beside me and we'll check out what's in the cloth wrapped package."

Yoshi knelt, careful not to spill the tea. He set the cup on the ground in front of them.

She untied the furoshiki and brought out a blue stoneware bowl of cold noodles, small chunks of cooked chicken and green vegetables on top. She set it on the ground next to the tea cup. Also inside the package were two sets of chopsticks in paper casings and two packets of sanitizing wipes.

Ritualistically they cleansed their hands and opened up their chopsticks.

"Okay." She picked up the cup, took a sip of the tea and handed the cup to him. "Sharing time begins."

****

A late afternoon shower swept across the mountains. They sat in the womb-like cave, eating their noodles, drinking tea, listening to the sound of the rain falling against the leaves, pattering on the stone path like slippered feet in a ballet. She watched Michio straighten up his quarters, which, as far as she could tell, didn't need straightening. Two shelves across the back held his cooking and serving utensils, a corner for his axe, straw broom, rake and water pail, another corner for his charcoal bag, a small cabinet for his meager food supplies and a bed of fragrant cedar boughs for his futon.

Was he still tortured by the disastrous events of his past, or had he set them aside—closed them off? His duties here might give him the security he needed, the penance he felt necessary. With his face pulled up into the warped smiling mask and his words few, how could anyone know his feelings. She had seen disfigurement before and not been affected but she found it difficult to look at Michio without wanting to cry.

The rain stopped after an hour. Michio took the pail in one hand, his cane in the other and tapped his way up to the spring. Upon returning, the pail full of water, he rolled up his futon and said in Japanese that his home was theirs for as long as they were here. He would spend his nights inside the shrine. He suggested they lay their futon on his cedar boughs and hoped their sleep would be restful.

They thanked him and watched him leave, the hollow tap-tap of his cane reverberating against the wet stone path as he made his way to the shrine.

It was after the cane tapping ceased that she and Yoshi emerged from the cave and stood by the boulder, surveying the effect of the sun's rays that pierced the clouds and shone like fire on the shrine. Pine needles turned silver. The air grew warm and carried a faint odor of incense. From a tree close by a bird warbled, answered by a bird from another limb and then another. A frog's deep croak echoed.

The fear and turmoil of the last few days was gone from her mind. She felt safe, protected. In a movement that seemed natural, she reached an arm around his waist.

He drew her body close to his side.

She responded by leaning her head on his shoulder. In San Francisco, caught in the legal rush, she found no time for the kind of serenity she felt now. In retrospect, none of her romances had been more than contrived situations, even with Eric. None had reached below the surface.

Until Yoshi.

Or was she getting carried away with the dream of what she wanted the relationship to be?

No, she assured herself, Yoshi was different from other men she had known. She respected his sensitivity, his straightforward, honest answers. She liked his gentle humor, his poetic nature, his intelligence, the determination he displayed to rescue her even when he must have been as frightened as she. His virtues were even more meaningful because she had the feeling he already knew her deeply and accepted the package, just as she knew and accepted him.

Not that she had opened up completely. She still walked a cautious line with Yoshi, distrustful that a serious relationship between a man and a woman could develop in only five days. Don't assume anything, she told herself. No leaps of faith. No quick judgments. No pouring out of emotions to be clobbered. And yet...and yet....

"Let's go to the other side," Yoshi said, gesturing, "I bet we can watch the sun set in the Japan Sea." He led her by the hand. "Yes, there it is."

Chelsea thought Michio must have often watched the sun set from there, as a bench stood at the point where the the wide sea spread below like a sheet of rippled gold. A few black dots moved slowly across the water. Pointing to a gray line in the distance, she asked, "Is that Korea?"

"I don't think so. It's the right direction, but the land is too far away. I think those are clouds."

They waited until the sky turned midnight blue and the sea velvet black before starting back to the cave, starlight to guide them, enough light only to see vague shapes.

At the cave entrance, she faced him, unable to discern his features. "What do you believe?"

"Are you asking me if I have a religion?"

"In a way, yes."

"That's an odd thing to ask me right now. I've never discussed it with anyone. Not sure I can put it into words."

She touched his hand. "Please try."

She could almost hear him thinking, could nearly touch his thoughts.

"Well, I don't go to a church," he began, "and I don't worship a god, although I understand how that helps some people. To me, it's a personal matter. I believe it's more important to revere than to worship."

"How do you see the difference?"

"To worship is a blind thing; to revere is to respect. Reverence is something you discover for yourself, not what you're told to do. What I revere most is the human spirit, especially when it's creative—a joining of ideas or things, making more than was there before." He paused. "I'm talking about creations that lift people up, not the sort that tear them down."

"There's a lot of tearing down these days."

"I know and yet *Dust as we are, the immortal spirit grows like harmony in music.*"

"That's a beautiful thought."

"It's from Wordsworth's 'Prelude'." He looked up at the stars. " I like Wordsworth and most poets of the Romantic Age. As they did, I feel a reverence for nature. To me, it's holy."

She wished for a sudden light to shine on him so she could be certain he was real.

"What about you?" he asked. "Tell me your beliefs?"

"I haven't thought about them for a long time. Not sure I still have any."

She reached up with both hands to explore his face, feeling the ridge of his nose, the wideness of his cheeks, the strength of his chin, the softness of his lips. "What about love, Yoshi? Do you believe in love?"

"I'd like to," he replied, "but I'm afraid."

"Why?"

"Because it might slip off my heart. Because I might be the only one who feels it now and if that is so, it will hurt too much."

"I'm just as afraid. I've watched love die. It happened with my mother and father. I've seen it vanish between friends. Sometimes I thought love came to me, but always it disappeared."

Her next words came out in a small voice. "Yoshi, if I give you my love, will you revere it?"

"Yes. Oh, yes."

"Then let's not be afraid."

CHAPTER 29

When Yoshi woke up the next morning, it took him a while to remember where he was. Japan. A mountain cave. Chelsea beside him. Memories of their love-making flooded though him and he felt an incredible joy.

She moaned in her sleep, then turned and nestled against him, her cheek on his chest, an arm stretched across his body. He felt her breasts rise and fall. A small flow of warm air from her mouth passed rhythmically over his bare chest. Running his hand though her prolific bangs, he smiled and wished all of life could be this simple, this beautiful.

But his left arm, caught beneath her body, was numb. Carefully he pried it out and worked his fingers until the circulation came back. From the direction of the shrine came the echoing tap-tap of the cane. He nudged her gently. "Michio's coming."

Her eyes flew open. She scrambled out of the futon and hastily pulled on her shirt. At the buttoning, she stopped. "I forgot. He can't see us."

Yoshi chuckled. "If he could, I doubt he'd mind."

She leaned over and kissed him. He pulled her back down onto the futon. The tapping came closer. Laughing, she pushed free and slipped on her underpants and slacks. "Even so, I can't greet anyone properly without my clothes on."

By the time Michio appeared at the cave entrance she was dressed. Yoshi, fascinated by watching her, had only managed to pull on his trousers. He finished dressing while the blind man moved to the charcoal stove, fanned the coals with a piece of bark until they glowed red, added charcoal from the corner bag and filled the brass kettle with water.

No hesitancy with his actions, Yoshi noticed. Michio knew where everything was, the exact distances in-between. Probably by the degree of heat, he knew when more charcoal was needed; by the weight of the kettle, when more water was necessary.

Yesterday Yoshi had found it painful to watch Michio drink tea, for the disfigured man was unable to close his lips over the cup, the tea dribbling down his chin, which he continually wiped with a small cloth he kept tucked in his sleeve. Yoshi wanted to give him a hug, tell him he was sorry, let him know he cared, but decided it might be mistaken for a show of pity, resulting in a loss of dignity, one of the few comforts Michio retained.

This morning during the tea drinking, Yoshi averted his eyes, repeating to himself over and over a line he remembered from "Childe Harold's Pilgrimage"—*for time and skill will couch the blind.* Yet, as hard as he tried to concentrate on the poem and stare into his cup, he could not escape the vision of Michio's white eyes and frozen smile and the tea dribbling down his chin.

When they were finished with the tea, Yoshi once more expressed in Japanese his gratitude for the hospitality. Politely, he inquired what sort of food his mother might bring and when they could expect her to come.

Michio replied haltingly that most often his mother brought broiled fish or chicken, but he could exist without either. Occasionally she brought her homemade *takuwan*, a long, thin radish turned mustard yellow that gave off a pungent smell Although appreciated, that was not necessary either. All he needed was rice and tea once a month, charcoal twice a year. Usually her arrival time was early in the day. Never this late.

Yoshi wondered how Michio recognized the time of day? His biological clock? Perhaps his blindness was not complete, and he could tell the difference between night and day.

He relayed Michio's information to Chelsea. She pressed her lips together and then spoke in a tight voice, "Wish we knew what was going on down there."

"Don't worry," Yoshi replied, trying to sound positive.

When no one came by mid-morning, Michio went to his storage cabinet and measured rice into a pan, seeming to know how much he'd poured out by the sound of the falling grains. He added water with a dipper and then covered the pan and steamed the rice on the charcoal burner. When the rice was done, Michio scooped out a rounded amount with a small wooden paddle and transferred it into the blue stoneware bowl Uncle Iiyama had given Chelsea. Over the top he sprinkled chopped green onions; Yoshi thought they must grow on the mountainside. From a jar of brine Michio pulled out a piece of takuwan. Michio sliced off five quarter-sized pieces and carefully arranged them in a semi-circle against the inner lip of the bowl as if creating a picture. Handing the bowl of rice to Yoshi, he explained that this was the first of two servings and asked if the chopsticks from yesterday had been saved. Yoshi assured him they were in the furoshiki, thanked him and passed the bowl on to Chelsea.

"*Oishii desu,*" said Chelsea, indicating the rice was delicious. "*Arigato.*"

Michio seemed surprised that Yoshi had allowed her to go first. "*Do itashimashite,*" Michio replied, his head bowed.

By noon Yoshi could no longer hide his concern. He told Michio he would go down the trail a short distance and meet his mother, who surely by now would be coming up the trail.

He set off, moving stealthily between the massive boulders and along the path, easier now without his suitcase. He was highly conscious of sounds. Not many. The birds had stopped singing. An occasional flutter in a bush or a whir of wings made him pause a moment to assess the sound. A rock slipped out from beneath his feet. He winced as it crackled down the ravine.

At the bench, he stopped, not daring to go further for fear of being seen from below. Remembering the ledge, he cautiously crawled over to it and stared down at the compound. No limousine. No sign of activity.

Crawling back to the bench, he sat there and considered what Chelsea and he should do if Michio's mother didn't come. They could stay another night at the shrine. What to eat? Rice, green onions, takuwan, and tea. Enough.

He frowned. But then what? They couldn't stay and continue to deplete Michio's supplies. Why didn't someone come to tell them what was happening? Had Kagawa tied up the family or locked them inside the studio or kidnapped them, drove them to wherever his boss Hayashi lurked or to some other yakuza hangout? Could they all be dead? No, Kagawa wouldn't do anything like that. It wouldn't help him find Chelsea and the valuable photos. Yet he might torture the family members, one by one, trying to get at the truth. Or yakuza might be hiding behind the rock spires by the hot pool, waiting for Chelsea to appear. Yoshi wiped the perspiration from his forehead. He must do something.

I'll wait until it's dark, he decided. Then I'll sneak down the trail. I'll find out what's going on. Yes, that's just what I'll do.

However, the thought of navigating the slippery trail at night alarmed him. For a moment he sat still, contemplating the dangers. I'll manage, he assured himself, sitting tall. I must. Once down there, I'll creep around the compound. I'll discover—

A crackling on the trail below.

Yoshi jumped up, alert, balancing on his toes. Not deer browsing. More like pebbles slipping off. He hid behind a tree and waited, his heart thumping like a distant drum. More crackles. Closer this time. He peeked out.

It was Michio's mother—the gray woman as Chelsea called her. In one hand she carried a furoshiki the same color as her black kimono. On her feet, jikatabi like Shunsuke wore.

Yoshi stepped out onto the trail.

Startled, she backed away. Realizing who it was, she nodded and gestured for him to move on ahead of her. They continued on to the shrine in silence.

The greeting between mother and son at the mouth of the cave was formal, both on their knees, bowing as if there was no sight problem. Ceremoniously, she opened the furoshiki and he accepted the broiled chicken and the takuwan as if they were sacred offerings. Rising, Michio returned to his shelf to store the food; his mother folded up the furoshiki and tucked it into the bosom of her kimono.

Yoshi understood their need for ritual but was anxious for the news. He noted Chelsea appeared even more impatient, rubbing her cheeks and nervously brushing back her bangs. Several times she adjusted her cross-legged position, her eyes darting back and forth between him and Michio's mother.

At last the woman spoke, her words in Japanese, her voice low and husky, sentences in fragments. When she was done, Yoshi translated the information to Chelsea. "Yesterday this frightful man with missing little fingers drove into the compound. While he searched the house, the three women and the little boy fled into the tatami room. Frightened, they huddled together and refused to speak. Then the man went into the warehouse, looking everywhere. He spoke with Uncle Iiyama and Shunsuke, who insisted they knew nothing about an American woman by the name of Chelsea Jarvis nor about a half Japanese man called Yoshi Moore. When Kagawa stated that Yoshi Moore was his nephew, Uncle Iiyama acted shocked and said he did not realize he had a nephew. Kagawa seemed satisfied and started to leave, but then he saw the cap on the porch. He picked it up and noticed the gold pin *CJ* inside. He remembered seeing the pin on Chelsea's hat."

"Oh, God," Chelsea gasped, "I took it off my hat and attached it to Toru's cap."

"I saw the cap on the porch," said Yoshi. "I should have reminded you to take it."

Michio's mother spoke again in Japanese, the words uttered slowly, her eyes closed. "This bad man knows you are here someplace. He looked very angry. He said, 'Miss Jarvis must bring the document to me today at 5:00. Meet me alone at Lafcadio Hearn's house.' Then he grabbed our little Hiro. He shoved the screaming boy into his limousine. He said, 'If she does not meet me with the envelope, you will never see your boy again.' He got into his big car and drove away."

She took a deep breath, blew it out forcibly and opened her eyes.

By the look on Chelsea's face, Yoshi realized she had understood it all.

Chelsea scrambled to her feet and cried, "If I don't meet him, Hiro will be killed."

Yoshi swallowed hard. He asked the woman why she hadn't come to the shrine earlier.

"Because of other men," she replied.

"Other men?"

The woman nodded. "After bad man go, other men come."

"Who?"

She shrugged. 'They talked to Uncle Iiyama. I not know who they are." Waving toward the path, her words now slipped over each other. "You hurry. Come. Leave suitcase and bag here. Shunsuke pick up later."

"Did you understand that?" he asked Chelsea.

"Yes," she replied and chewed on her lower lip. She pulled the manila envelope out of her bag and stuffed it down the front of her shirt. "But I don't understand who the other men are."

"Could be government agents," said Yoshi. "We'll get the details from Uncle Iiyama."

They said their good-byes and thank-yous to Michio. The woman spoke something soft and unintelligible to her son and they touched hands before she abruptly turned and led the way out of the cave. Michio followed them as far as the torii.

Before passing between the boulders, Yoshi turned for a last look. In the center of the gate, Michio stood with his cane, his body tense as if listening to their departure, his scars vivid in the sunlight. He must have been aware of Yoshi's eyes on him, for he executed a farewell bow.

Yoshi bowed back.

CHAPTER 30

Chelsea and Yoshi hurried around the side of the warehouse. Uncle Iiyama stood in the center of the compound talking to Midori while Shunsuke hitched the ox to the cart

"Ah," cried Uncle Iiyama, striding toward them. "You made good time down the mountain."

Chelsea said, "Came as fast as we could. What's happened? Who were the other men?"

"All will be well," insisted the uncle.

"But what about Hiro?" asked Yoshi.

Midori burst into tears. Shunsuke took her by the arm and led her toward the house. The gray woman, head down, shuffled after them.

"*Do mo arigato,*" Chelsea called after her but the old woman didn't turn around.

Uncle Iiyama watched her disappear inside. "She heard you, Miss Jarvis, but somehow she has lost the desire to say 'you are welcome.'" He patted the ox's head. "There is no need to rush. Let us sit on the porch a few minutes while I bring you up to date on what has happened."

Chelsea frowned. "Why can't we talk about it on the oxcart? Let's get going."

"We have time," said the uncle, leading the way.

"But—"

"Please, Miss Jarvis, before we go, a discussion is necessary."

After they were seated on the porch, he said, "You must tell Mr. Kagawa that you will go with him to the airport and—"

Chelsea jumped up. "What? I'm not going to carry this damn thing through customs. The deal is this: Kagawa gets the envelope only if he releases Hiro."

"No, Miss Jarvis," Uncle Iiyama said with equal force. "There has been a change. Mr. Kagawa will not let Hiro go unless you agree to deliver the envelope to their agent in San Francisco."

She threw up her hands in despair. "I can't do that."

"Yes, yes, I know, but you must *say* you will. And you must find a way for him to *take* the envelope. Explain that it's for safety reasons until the airport. By doing this, you will be instrumental in his undoing."

She folded her arms, sat down and waited for an explanation.

Ayako arrived with a tray of tea and a plate of what looked like tiny dumplings. She set the tray on the railing, bowed and went back into the house.

Uncle Iiyama said, "I asked Ayako to bring us tea and *wagashi*, tea sweets, before we set out for Matsue." He gestured at the plate. "This particular kind of tea sweet is *mochi*." He handed them each a cup of tea and then offered Chelsea the plate of rice cakes.

"This is all quite charming," said Chelsea with a touch of sarcasm, "but I can't imagine why you force us to sit here drinking tea and eating mochi when Hiro has been kidnapped and I face a possible disaster."

The uncle stiffened. "Believe me, I care deeply about you and Hiro. However, it is important to understand matters before flying into the fray." He offered the plate to Yoshi, who quickly picked up a mochi.

With a sigh of resignation Chelsea reached over and took one of the cakes. She plopped it into her mouth, surprised at the sweetness of the paste inside.

Uncle Iiyama set the plate on the tray. "Now that we are under control, I will tell you what has occurred." He sat down, sipped his tea and nibbled on his rice cake.

Chelsea wasn't sure if Uncle Iiyama was playing mind games with her or determined to handle the matter in his traditional manner. She regretted her earlier burst and decided to attempt a calm demeanor.

The uncle said, "Following Mr. Kagawa's departure two security guards arrived."

"Government security?" Chelsea softly inquired.

"No, guards hired by a major corporation."

"Which one?"

"I'm not free to say. But I can tell you that the material in the envelope was stolen from this corporation. With your help, the thief can be arrested and the envelope confiscated."

Chelsea reached for another rice cake. "What happens to the envelope's contents?'

"They are to be destroyed. It is not necessary to know why." He cleared his throat and went on. "What is important for you to know is that the moment Mr. Kagawa takes the envelope he can be arrested. Then you will be free of this unfortunate business." Uncle Iiyama smiled, no mirth in his eyes.

Chelsea frowned. "You say these guards came last night?"

"Yes, shortly after Mr. Kagawa left?"

"Then, why didn't Michio's mother come to the shrine early this morning? I was told that was her usual custom."

His eyes narrowed. "We cannot always follow customs." He put his cup down, rose and strolled toward the oxcart.

They set their cups on the tray and hurried after him.

Uncle Iiyama climbed onto the cart, Chelsea pulled up next to him and Yoshi came in beside her. The three perched on the front board, their feet resting on a narrow trough below it.

The uncle said to Chelsea, "You may wonder why I use this simple means of transportation."

"It does seem odd, especially since you have such a hi-tech communication base."

"I use an oxcart because the gray lady, as you call her, associates trucks with her husband's death and her son Michio's disfigurement. It is a small concession to help quell her fear." He made a clicking sound and slapped the reins on the ox's back. The cart creaked past the hot springs, around the monster rocks and through the stunted conifers.

The day was warm. Chelsea stared at a paddy sheeted with water. At one end, a row of people in conical straw hats like Uncle Iiyama's moved slowly forward, bent over, ankle-deep in the water, inserting rice plants.

Yoshi put an arm around her. "I should be with you when you meet Kagawa."

She shook her head. "I must go alone. It's a requirement."

Uncle Iiyama said, "The moment he accepts the envelope, the arrest will be made."

"What if Hiro isn't with him?" Yoshi asked.

"He will be," replied the uncle. "The boy is his bargaining chip."

Chelsea squeezed Yoshi's hand. "Everything's going to be fine," she whispered, trying to exude a confidence she didn't feel.

They approached the main road, as empty as two days ago. Turning toward the city, they rode on, the clip-clop of the ox's hooves sounding more like the ticking of an old, abandoned clock. It seemed increasingly necessary for her to get answers before the ticking stopped.

"These security guards," she said, "have they been tailing Mr. Kagawa?"

"One has. The other followed you from Okayama."

She blinked. "You mean he was on the train?"

"Yes, he spoke to you both."

"The student," breathed Yoshi. "How did he know where we were?"

Uncle Iiyama examined the reins before answering. "Uncle Nagata told the Tokyo Police."

"Ah," said Chelsea, "so now it's a police operation and corporation's guards are no longer involved."

The uncle waved an arm as if to brush away a fly. "They are still involved."

"How come?"

"It's the nature of the material," he snapped.

After a sideways glance at her, the uncle continued in a moderated voice, "Last night I called the Tokyo Police. I didn't receive details until mid-morning which is why Midori's mother was late to the shrine."

Yoshi frowned. "Great Uncle Nagata must have known we were being followed."

"Yes. I spoke with him on the phone the day you arrived. He was relieved."

"Why?" pressed Chelsea.

Uncle Iiyama gave her a stern look. "In our country, Miss Jarvis, it is natural to be concerned about the welfare of a relative and his friend."

"I mean why did the guy follow us? You know more about this than you're telling us."

Uncle Iiyama reined in the ox to allow a group of children to cross the road. "Excuse me, Miss Jarvis, you are too persistent. I do not wish to say any more about this matter."

"Well, I do," cried Chelsea. She leaned forward, attempting to get the uncle to look at her. "I have the right to know why I'm doing something dangerous."

"All you need to know," the uncle said, his voice rising, "is that Mr. Kagawa is a thief who will be caught." He tapped the reins on the ox and the cart moved forward again.

The only sounds were the creaking of the cart and the clopping of the ox's hooves. Yoshi tightened his hold on Chelsea's arm.

After a while the uncle said, "We come from different cultures, Miss Jarvis. There are conflicting interests here—face-saving ones shall we say."

"Okay, but Yoshi is your nephew and I'm his good friend. Why must you be so secretive with us?"

Stroking his mustache and beard, Uncle Iiyama studied her face. "I'm sorry. Most sorry. My belief is that I can trust only the members of my family who live in my country."

They rode on, the silence rapidly building a stronger barrier.

Abruptly Yoshi spoke, his voice loud and defiant. "Uncle Iiyama, if what you wish is a pledge of secrecy, we'll give it to you. Let me assure you, a pledge carries as much weight for us as it does in your country." His voice fell away. "Which I'd hoped would be partly mine."

The uncle leaned forward as if surprised. "I cannot be sure of you."

Yoshi raised his chin. "You think because we're foreigners we can't be trusted. Well, maybe we can't trust you either. Maybe nobody should trust anybody."

"Maybe not," the uncle shot back. "When I was twelve, Uncle Nakata's wife and their two daughters were killed at Hiroshima. I saw the devastation, heard tales of horror from my relatives. Many years later, a tall American soldier came to our country for a rest while fighting another war—Vietnam. My sister married him. I still find it hard to believe she did such a thing."

"That was long ago," Yoshi said quietly. "Isn't it time we end the war?"

The uncle closed his eyes and turned away.

The ox plodded on, the cart creaking past a group of women who walked along the side of the road, all carrying bundles on their backs. Two bicyclists zinged their handlebar bells and rode by. Ahead a truck stopped to let out a passenger. Chelsea watched the city inch closer. On the hill, Matsue Castle loomed dark and foreboding.

Just as she had given up all hope of learning any more, Uncle Iiyama released a long, loud sigh. "I will take the chance," he said. "Promise me you will say nothing of this to anyone."

They promised.

When the road was empty of people, Uncle Iiyama continued. "Although most yakuza, in spite of their underworld dealings, tend to be patriotic, one syndicate is headed by a ruthless man, Mr. Hayashi, whose only concerns are accumulating wealth and power. I do not consider him Japanese. It was he who arranged for the incriminating photos to be taken for blackmail. Several days ago Uncle Nagata told the Tokyo Police Chief about them." He paused and stared at Chelsea as if weighing the the value of revealing more.

Chelsea stared back unflinching. Yoshi met his uncle's eyes.

After another deep sigh, the uncle went on, "This morning the Chief told me that his electronic surveillance experts had located and destroyed the digital chip that carried the photos. Through an informant, the Chief learned that only one set of prints was made of the photos. You, Miss Jarvis have them."

Chelsea touched her chest to be assured the envelope was still there.

The uncle continued, "A particular corporation was asked to allege the prints were stolen from their files so an arrest could be made on Mr. Kagawa."

"I see," said Chelsea. "Unless the material was stolen, an arrest could not be made. A man does not commit a crime by simply possessing photos."

"Kidnapping Hiro is a crime," said Yoshi.

"That situation didn't develop until yesterday," Uncle Iiyama reminded him.

Chelsea said, "I don't understand why the corporation agreed to assist in this operation?"

"Several years ago, Mr. Kagawa worked for the company. He was fired. They believed he stole and peddled their secrets but were unable to prove it."

"So, this was a chance to finally catch their thief."

"Yes. All has been accomplished in utmost secrecy. And," he emphasized, "it must remain so." He studied Chelsea. "Perhaps in your country the matter would be handled differently?"

She looked down, thinking it probably would be. Most likely in America the content of the envelope would be leaked out, blasted onto TV, the pictures posted on YouTube. Reporters would hound the two men. There would be a congressional investigation, the CIA involved. Relations between Japan and the U.S. could be deeply affected by the scandal.

"I'm surprised the Police Chief gave you all this information," she said.

"He trusted me."

"Why should he?"

"Because he is my father."

"Your father!" exclaimed Yoshi. "Good grief!"

"Yes. Your grandfather, Tsuyoshi. Your grandmother's husband. And the head of the corporation is—" He broke off, glanced at Chelsea and Yoshi and then focused on the road ahead.

Chelsea said, "I gather you're reluctant to tell us who heads the assisting corporation."

Still staring ahead, he blurted out, "It is the brother of Michio's and Midori's mother."

"The gray woman's brother?"

"Yes."

They had reached the outskirts of Matsue. Uncle Iiyama guided the ox into a right turn, taking the same narrow road they had traveled on their way out of the city. During the slow climb up the hill, they passed people who nodded greetings.

Chelsea took a deep breath and let the air out slowly. Her hands were sweaty. She wiped them on the sides of her trousers.

Uncle Iiyama reined in the ox. The cart was three quarters up the hill. "This is as far as we go with you," he said quietly. "Lafcadio Hearn's house is around that corner, close to the castle."

She shook Uncle Iiyama's hand. "Whatever happens, your secret is safe with me."

Yoshi jumped from the cart and helped her down. They embraced quickly. She squeezed his cold hands, smiling with assurance and then walked up the empty street, holding the envelope in front of her, the broken wax seal toward her body.

CHAPTER 31

As Chelsea turned the corner she saw the sign in front of the Lafcadio Hearn house. On the next street over stood Matsue Castle with Kagawa's black limousine parked by the drawbridge. The only people in sight were three Japanese men; they snapped pictures of the Hearn house before disappearing inside.
Were they the police? Or were they not here?

Kagawa stepped out of his car. He peered up and down the street before opening the back door and pulling out Hiro. He leaned over and spoke to the boy who wiped his eyes and took Kagawa's hand. They walked toward Chelsea.

Chelsea proceeded, focusing on the muscular man she so thoroughly disliked. A few feet in front of him she stopped. "*Konnichi wa, Kagawa-san.*"

"*Konnichi wa,*" he grunted and reached for her arm.

She pulled away. "We need to talk."

He glanced around. "We have nothing to discuss."

"My concern is that you won't keep your word. I mean, about letting the boy go and depositing the money in my bank account."

"My word is my honor," he replied, raising his chin.

"Looks like I'll have to believe you." She glared at him. "So, we head for the airport. Let the boy go. His uncle waits down the hill." For Hiro's benefit she pointed in the direction.

"Where is your briefcase?" Kagawa asked.

She swallowed. "With my suitcase. I left them in a locker at the Odawara train station." She hoped to God they had lockers. "I plan to pick them up on my way back."

He studied the envelope in her hand and then looked at Hiro whose face was wrinkling up as if he were trying hard not to cry.

Chelsea repeated softly, "Let the boy go." She held out the envelope, wax seal down. "And keep this until we reach the airport."

"You keep it for now."

She raised her eyebrows. "Before, when you traveled with me, you insisted the envelope stay with you. Have you lost concern for its safety?"

"Of course not. For now, though, I wish you to carry it."

Hiro began to sniffle. "I want to go home," he whined.

"Hush," Kagawa hissed, looking around, "or I'll never let you go."

Hiro trembled, tears sliding down his cheeks.

Kagawa said, "Miss Jarvis, I will release the boy after you are inside the car."

"Okay, I'm ready." Chelsea grasped Kagawa's free hand. She dropped the envelope to the street. Holding his hand tightly, she said, "Sorry. I'm nervous."

Kagawa let go of Hiro and picked up the envelope.

"Run," Chelsea cried.

Hiro took off down the hill like a rocket.

With a grunt of annoyance, Kagawa pushed Chelsea toward the car. "No more tricks. Get in!"

From behind the limousine two Japanese men rushed out. One—Chelsea recognized the student from the train—snapped a picture of Kagawa and jumped into the back seat of the car. The other leaped in behind the wheel. As the limousine sped away, Kagawa yelled and lurched after it, stuffing the envelope inside his shirt and dragging Chelsea along. She struggled against his grip.

The three men charged from Hearn's house, their guns drawn. In Japanese they shouted for Kagawa to halt and raise his hands. Chelsea broke free. Kagawa caught her by the arm, his hold like an iron clamp. He whipped out a knife from his left sleeve and held it against her throat.

Two more men, their revolvers aimed at Kagawa, ran from behind nearby bushes. Kagawa and the five men shouted back and forth in Japanese. Chelsea understood none of it, her arm caught in a vise, the edge of the blade pressed against her throat so she could scarcely breathe. Holding her in front of him, Kagawa backed up toward the castle drawbridge, still yelling at the men. In the distance she saw Yoshi rushing toward them. Kagawa bellowed something. All lowered their weapons. Yoshi stopped, his face full of horror. "Don't do it," he shouted.

She closed her eyes, terrified. Kagawa's going to kill me, she thought.

"We go into the castle donjon," Kagawa snarled at her in English, his breath hot against her cheek.

"Take away the knife," she whispered. "I'll go with you."

The steel pressed tighter. "Follow my directions. Do not struggle."

Her neck pulsed against his blade, hammering faster with each beat. They backed across the bridge, through the gate, onto the empty castle grounds.

The police must have cleared everyone from the area, she thought. Why were they allowing Kagawa to hold her hostage? Perhaps it didn't matter if a foreign woman was killed. The castle was sealed off. Kagawa couldn't stay inside forever; eventually they would recover their valuable document. She was expendable.

As her captor dragged her backward to the donjon, she counted the half circles of split bamboo fence that lined the path, their ends forced into the ground in an overlapping pattern, loop upon loop, like the paper chains she made as a child. Trees overhung the path, shrubs shrouded the grounds, the sky vanished. He's pulling me toward my grave, she thought. "Yoshi," she whispered. "Yoshi." She couldn't see him anymore. Couldn't see the police. All gone. Deserted by everyone.

Inside the donjon, Kagawa thrust her aside and commanded, "Wait there." He left her at the foot of the winding stairway.

She rubbed her bruised arm and gingerly touched her neck. Her heart beat too hard, too fast.

He pulled shut the heavy donjon door. The room turned dark, dungeon-like, the smell musty. He drew the iron bolt across the door.

She tried to think but her thoughts were shattered. Her body trembled. "I'm going to die," she murmured over and over again.

"We go to the top," he said. She obeyed, climbing the narrow, steep stairs as if hypnotized. Now and then she glanced back. He followed, walking with his elbows-out, chin-jutting manner.

They reached the second flight, the third, the fourth. At the top was the smallest room, the brightest—more windows and an open doorway leading to an encircling balcony. Clean, cool air. She grabbed the balcony railing and breathed in deeply.

He removed the manila envelope from his jacket and turned it over, touching the seal. "It is broken," he said, a catch in his voice. Closing his eyes, he beat on his chest and cried to the sky, "I have failed. Failed!"

Surprised, her trembling stopped. The fresh air helped clear her mind, brought strength back to her body. She followed him into the room.

He knelt in the center and set the envelope on the floor, his dagger on top like a paper weight. In a shaky voice, he said, "I did not accomplish the most important assignment ever given to me by my master."

She noted how she would have to walk around him to get to the stairway.

He took off his jacket and spread it on the floor, then drew out another dagger strapped to his right arm and set it beside his jacket. He unfastened the two weapon straps. Next he removed his tie. Folding the items neatly, he placed them by the stairway railing.

Better to run behind him him, she decided.

As though cognizant of her thoughts he said quietly, "Wait, please. I need you as a witness."

His polite manner perplexed her. Something about the way he slowly unbuttoned his shirt held her attention. When he removed the shirt she was shocked, fascinated by the intricate tattoos that covered his upper body and arms—red peonies swirling around cranes and a mountain stream. He knelt there, majestic, muscles taut, the designs on his skin looking like an elegant screen wrapped tightly around his body. She found it hard to reconcile the thug she hated with the man who now knelt before her.

In a ritualistic manner he folded his shirt and set it with the other three items. Sitting cross-legged on his jacket, he picked up his dagger and held it out before him, blade pointing inward.

She gasped, "What are you going to do?"

"I shall commit *seppuku.*"

"Suicide? You can't. It's ridiculous."

"It is honorable," he said calmly. "I have not lived up to my master's expectations."

"You don't have to live up to anybody's expectations. You live in a free world."

"I must make a cut," he said to himself as if practicing his maneuvers, "from here," he touched an area to the left below his ribs, "to here," he drew the line diagonally down to the right. "Then, thrust my blade into the center. Eventually I will die, but it will be a slow death, with incredible pain." He looked up into her eyes. "I know how much you dislike me, Miss Jarvis. I have no right to ask anything of you, or to think you would wish to help me. Yet I believe you are a kind woman. Therefore, I ask you one favor. When I have finished the cut, take my other dagger and sever the carotid artery in my neck." He pointed to the place with the tip of his knife. "It will kill me instantly and stop my suffering."

"I can't do that," she cried. "It would be a criminal act. You don't have to kill yourself. You owe nothing to Hayashi. He took advantage of your loyalty. If you tell what you know about this blackmail business, the police will protect you. You'll get a light sentence. I'm lawyer. I know about such things. Put that knife down. Give yourself up."

"You do not understand," he said.

A pounding echoed up the stairway. Through the doorway she heard men's voices in the courtyard below.

She said, "Give me the knife, Kagawa-san. Please, give me the knife."

"Keep away from me." He plunged the dagger into his body and drew the cut. Blood oozed out in a red stream. A tangled rope of intestines spilled onto the floor. His back held erect, he stared ahead, his face contorted in pain.

She shrieked and backed away. Turning, she started to run down the stairs. He groaned. She stopped, turned and stared at his tortured face.

"I'm sorry," she whispered. "I don't want to see you suffer. But I can't do what you ask." Once again she started to go, then stopped, his face imprinted on her mind. Tears streamed down her cheeks. She couldn't run away and leave him this way. She had to help. She had to.

Picking up the other dagger, she knelt in front of him. He reached out and touched her cheek, his eyes pleading. She took a deep breath and with a quick thrust severed the artery. He fell forward into her arms, pushing her backwards. A wail rose from deep inside her. Sobbing, she dropped the knife and struggled to hold him, blood splattering.

The pounding on the door below increased. More shouting and banging.

At last her tears stopped. With a great effort she managed to push the lifeless Kagawa off of her. She picked up his shirt and wiped as best she could the blood from his tattooed body and face.

Carrying the blood-soaked shirt like an offering, she started down the stairs. On the third flight she stumbled catching herself. The beating on the door and the yelling voices came from another world. She continued on down until she reached the ground floor and the great iron door where she fumbled with the bolt, struggled with all her might and pushed it back, her bloody hands slippery, the shirt wadded up. At last the bolt grated across. The door burst open. The police rushed through the doorway. "The photos?" asked one.

"Up there," she whispered.

The police charged up the stairs.

Yoshi came through the doorway and drew her into his arms. He guided her out into the courtyard. She stared at the bamboo half circles that lined the pathway, dropped Kagawa's blood-soaked shirt onto one of them and in a faltering voice said, "Why? Why did he have to do it?"

"Perhaps he thought he was a samurai," Yoshi said. "Whatever the reason, it's all over. You're safe now." He led her down the hill toward the oxcart where Hiro was huddled in Uncle Iiyama's lap.

Yoshi helped her onto the cart bench and climbed up beside her. Uncle Iiyama slapped the reins. The ox pulled the creaking cart around facing downhill and started home.

"I killed him," Chelsea said, her voice weary. "I couldn't bear to see him suffer."

"He was dying anyway," said Yoshi.

Uncle Iiyama nodded. "What you did was honorable."

"I'm not sure what honorable means; I do know that legally what I did was wrong."

CHAPTER 32

On the train ride from Matsue to Okayama, Yoshi held Chelsea in his arms, his warmth comforting. He explained why the police hadn't immediately come to her rescue at the castle. The shouting back and forth between Kagawa and the police, the words she hadn't understood, her mind too freaked out to translate: Kagawa said he wouldn't hurt the woman and asked for time to take care of himself; the police demanded assurance; Kagawa promised, claiming it a matter of honor; the police finally believed him and allowed him the time he needed.

Toru and Kayako met them in Okayama, bringing along Chelsea's suitcase and hat. They drove Yoshi and Chelsea to the train station in Osaka, where they said goodbye and promised to communicate often. Yoshi then bought two Bullet Train tickets to Kyoto and made a call to the inn where he and Chelsea had met. He reserved a room for two nights.

When they arrived at the inn, the bald-headed man in the foyer smiled in recognition of their shoes. At the front desk, the lady who had served them dinner and secreted the note from Yoshi to Chelsea greeted them as if they were returning relatives, bowing low and blowing a welcome kiss.

The next afternoon, Yoshi took Chelsea to his grandmother's house. Yoshi wore the blue kimono Uncle Iiyama had given him, Chelsea the hand-painted kimono with a crane design, a parting gift from Midori and Shunsuke. On their feet were tabi and zori, gifts from Kayako and Toru. They rang the bell at the gate and then walked into the front garden.

Grandmother, in a pearl gray kimono, a darker gray obi around her waist, waited at the open shoji screen, her head bowed. They slipped off their zori and entered her room. Yoshi smoothly shut the shoji behind him and deposited an envelope on her low table, his contribution to defray the tea expenses. "Customary for a formal ceremony," he whispered to Chelsea. Grandmother nodded and handed them each a small black fan, Yoshi's was slightly larger.

"What do I do with it?" Chelsea asked him in a hushed voice, not wanting to embarrass him or insult Grandmother by doing the wrong thing.

"Carry it with you but don't open it," he replied softly. "After you enter the teahouse, set the fan on the tatami before you."

Grandmother withdrew two small paper packets from a sleeve of her kimono. "Tissues," she said, "for finger wiping," and she motioned how the fan and the packet could be carried tucked into the kimono. Shuffling across the room to her garden shoji, she indicated three pair of zori on the outside landing.

They slipped their feet into the sandals and Grandmother gestured for them to walk in front of her. "We go to waiting place," she told them, closing the shoji behind her.

The path was a combination of stepping stones and small gravel, lined with colorful flowers including peonies. The cherry tree by the pond was in full bloom, radiantly pink as if glowing from an inner light. After the path curved, they passed through a gate and the garden took on a quieter tone—no flowering plants. Instead, trees, shrubs and rocks in simple shapes.

Nestled in an arbor near the teahouse, in a cooler garden of ferns and moss was a wooden bench with round straw cushions. Beside it on a nearby post, a hand-made broom hung from a hook. In front of the arbor was a low, stone basin with a long-handled wooden dipper resting across its top.

They sat on the bench, Chelsea between Yoshi and Grandmother. No one spoke. Grandmother closed her eyes as if meditating.

Chelsea heard a slight clacking at the side of the teahouse. A door about four feet square slid open, and Great Uncle Nagata, carrying a wooden bucket, crawled through. Without a sign of acknowledgment, he walked to the stone basin and crouched on the flat, raised rock in front of it, picking up the dipper. With the bucket held to his left side, he drew water from it, sprinkling around the area. He dipped out more water to cleanse his hands and rinse out his mouth. The rest of the water he poured into the basin, some overflowing, wetting the sides of the stone.

Rising, he faced the three. They rose and bowed. He bowed back. Carrying his bucket, he returned to the teahouse and crawled through the entrance, sliding the door shut behind him. The three again sat down on the bench. After a few moments, Grandmother looked at Yoshi, who stood and approached the stone basin. Chelsea started to get up, but the slight raising of Grandmother's hand told her to wait. When Yoshi was finished with his purification, he walked toward the teahouse.

Grandmother nodded to Chelsea. Remembering Yoshi's instructions to imitate the rituals he performed, she approached the stone basin and followed his same ablutions, her motions just as deliberate and slow. When finished, she walked after Yoshi, keeping a distance between them and staying back as he knelt on a flat stone at the teahouse entrance. He slid open the small door to the building. Removing his zori, he deposited them next to Great Uncle Nagata's. Then he crawled inside. She sensed Grandmother was coming behind her.

After following Yoshi's procedures, Chelsea entered the teahouse on her hands and knees. It was a small room only three tatami wide but the ceiling was tall. Yoshi now stood before an alcove, then knelt. He bowed and appeared to admire the hanging scroll with *kanji* written on it—a wise saying, she imagined. Beneath the *kanji* scroll was an incense burner on a packet of papers.

Uncle Iiyama wasn't in the room. Noting another entrance beside the alcove, she figured he must be making preparations for the tea ceremony.

Yoshi rose and walked to the right. She heard a rustle behind her. Grandmother came through the entrance.

Chelsea stood up as gracefully as possible and moved to the alcove, where she knelt and bowed in Yoshi's manner. She studied the scroll, clearing her mind of thoughts. Rising, she moved on, Grandmother taking her place.

By the time she knelt to the left of Yoshi and placed the fan before her on the tatami, a deep quiet had settled over her.

Great Uncle Iiyama entered from the door by the alcove. He brought in the implements and ingredients to be used in the tea ceremony. Patiently, she waited for the ancient ritual to begin, her body relaxed, her mind eased from the horrors and fears of the past week.

CHAPTER 33

Three days after the tea ceremony, Chelsea sat at her desk in the law office. Half an hour until the doors opened, the phones still on answering service and nobody else around. Soon they would all pour in, calling greetings, picking up messages, checking calendars, secretaries examining files—the start of the legal bustle of the day.

She looked through her window at the fog-shrouded court house, its monumental dome so familiar that she had a moment of doubt she had been away from it. The emotions of that horrible afternoon at Matsue's castle were fading, the bad dreams nearly gone, except for a frightening face—Kagawa's—that at times woke her up. She still felt conflicted over what she had done—breaking open a client's private envelope and ending a dying man's life. Did she believe her acts were justified? She thought so but wasn't sure. Might there be other times when she would not follow the letter of the law?

When she heard about the arrest of Hayashi and his gang and the confiscation of illegal documents from his corporation, she dismissed her fear that the yakuza might be after her, although she wished they could have caught Eric, who had managed to disappear. Yoshi had learned all of this before they left Japan through a phone conversation with his grandfather, who, in spite of his advanced age, was the revered Chief of the Tokyo Police Force. "But he refused to meet me," Yoshi said. "Seems as if the the wound of losing his daughter to an American soldier has never healed."

Saying goodbye to Yoshi at the Narita Airport had been hard. They clung to each other until the last boarding call for her plane. She loved him; didn't want to lose him. Yet how could she hold him? He must fly back to Seattle to continue as an English professor at the University of Washington, and she must return to San Francisco to carry on with her law practice. Their lives didn't fit together. It had been a wonderful love affair. Best to forget him she tried to tell herself on the flight home, although she knew she never would.

The intercom buzzed. Chelsea glanced at her watch: nine a.m. First call of the day. She swiveled her chair around from the window, pushed down the button, and asked the receptionist, "Who is it?"

"A gentleman on line three. Refuses to give his name. Insists it's urgent."

Eric flashed through her mind. Her body tensed; her hands turned cold. Vigorously she rubbed her fingers together and picked up her ballpoint pen. "I'll take the call," she said and lifted the phone receiver, cradling it on her right shoulder. She pushed line three. "This is Chelsea Jarvis," she said crisply. "How may I help you?"

"In many ways," said a familiar voice.

"Yoshi!" She dropped her pen. It rolled across the desk and into the waste basket.

"Are you all right?" he asked.

"Yeah, yeah, fine. And you?"

"Not bad but I miss you."

"I miss you, too," she said.

"I don't know how I'm going to make it through the next month and a half."

She caught her breath. "What happens then?"

"I'm teaching a summer course practically next door to you. In Berkeley, at the University of California."

Her eyes lit up. "Terrific!" She laughed. "That's my alma mater."

"Then I'll treat it with respect."

"Of course. That's how you treat everything." Her voice caught. "And everyone."

There was a pause. She pressed her ear tightly against the earpiece.

"*Itsumo maemukini,*" he said at last.

"What's that mean?"

"Always looking forward."

"Are you?"

"Am I what?"

"Always looking forward."

"Yes, I'm like a tiger beating the drum. I'm going to find a way for us to be together. I don't want to lose you."

She buried the receiver in a kiss. "Don't want to lose you either."

The intercom buzzed. A light flashed on line four.

"Nuts," she said. "I'm getting another call."

"I'll phone you tonight," he said. "By the way, my mother's going to Japan next month. She's determined to see Grandfather, taking along a haiku I wrote for him." In a shy voice he added, "I wrote a poem for you too, sort of an ode. Not a good one, but here it is:

> Let us weave our dreams together
> Until the stars shine no more.
>   Chelsea, Chelsea, my love,
>   So cries my heart."

On his end, the receiver clicked. Her body seemed to rise above her chair. She floated with Yoshi on a lake filled with water lilies; he took her hand and they flew to the top of Mt. Fuji.

The receptionist buzzed again.

"Yes?" she answered vaguely.

"It's Mrs. Thompson on line four. She's worried about the trial."

With a supreme effort Chelsea brought her mind back into the office. She pushed line three off and line four on.

"Hello, Mrs. Thompson," she said in her lawyer voice. "There's no need to worry. Everything's completely under control."

THE END

FAMILY TREE OF YOSHI'S ANCESTORS
USING NAMES THAT APPEAR IN THE BOOK

LEGEND:
= married
(d) deceased
| offspring

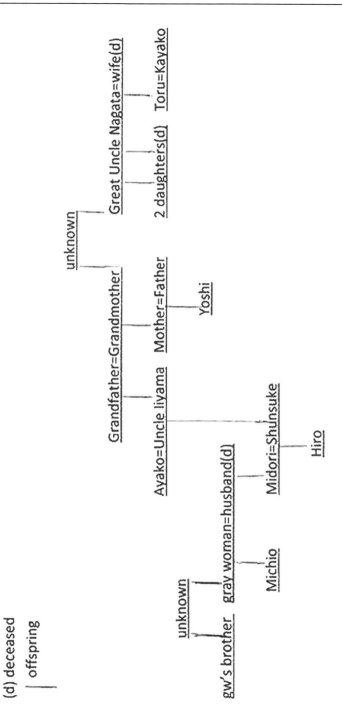

ACKNOWLEDGMENTS

My deepest thanks to consultant Eiko Iritani and editor Kathryn Keve.

Also, thanks to the following people for their help and encouragement: Professor Hiro Kawasaki, Bill Calderhead, sculptors Duncan Y. McKiernan and Phillip Levine and members of my writer's group Michael J. Smith, Brett Gadbois, D.L. Fowler, Laurie Ezpeleta and Marcia Rudoff. Other who presented good ideas in the early days of the manuscript's creation were Yumiko and Matthew Kott, Noni Kott, David Kragen, Venera Barles and Nancy Rekow.

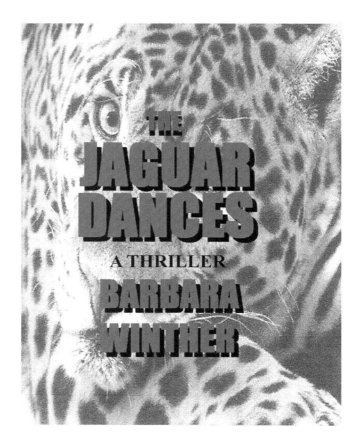

THE JAGUAR DANCES, the first in a trio of thrillers that involves women associated with the San Francisco law office of McCloskey, Warner & Jarvis, is about what happens when Jan, McCloskey's secretary, travels to Peru with her friend Carrie for a relaxing vacation and instead becomes embroiled in a wild affair ,

Reviews

In Winther's thriller, a vacation goes perilously awry when two friends encounter danger, intrigue and drug smugglers in the exotic resorts and mountain villages of Peru...Winther nicely ramps up the suspense and tension from page to page, and her details of Peru's landscape, natives and locales pull readers into a lush South American realm...An ultimately fulfilling thriller with plenty of treachery, villains and heroes to go around.
Kirkus Reviews

Barbara Winther infuses this fast paced novel of adventure and intrigue with a wonderful sense of place. Two young women vacation in Peru, but the itinerary soon includes mystery, romance and danger. This is a page-turner that is hard to put down, and I'm eager for more!
Barbara Tolliver, The Traveler Store

The golden eye of the Jaguar haunts two young women out for a holiday. At every step, they find challenges never faced in their routines at home. The jaguar is an apt symbol of the danger and resolve that shadow Jan and Carrie in Winther's fascinating thriller.
Kathryn Keve, Editing and Publishing Services

A dramatic portrait of Peru. Winther leads us through an intricate dance as Jaguar, the ancient symbol of power and oppression, shows its modern face in this struggle for political domination and personal control over destiny.
Richard Kinsman, Public Television Art Director (retired)

I liked the short chapters which suited my concentration level. The author's obvious acquaintance with Peru and its language nuances are self-evident. No point to travel there as the book truly caught the atmosphere! I was impressed with the eye for detail. I could practically hear the squeaking of the damn luggage cart belonging to Carrie. The book covered all the essentials for a thriller. I found it most realistic and definitely readable. Some film producer should get interested in this story.
Peter Martin, Language Consultant and teacher of English as a foreign language

As an avid reader of "thrillers," particularly in the genre of what goes on in and about other countries, the book was both informative, exciting and with great plot and three-dimensional characters. There was such a lovely rhythm to the flow of the story, between action and observation. Stylistically, it moved along at an enjoyable pace. The most simple way to state it, is, that it is very readable and well written.
Phillip Levine, a prominent Pacific Northwest sculptor

THE LEOPARD SINGS, the second installment of Winther's thriller series involving women related to the San Francisco law office of McCloskey, Warner and Jarvis, follows Warner and his wife, Allison to Kenya on a vacation that turns deadly, capped by two terrifying days that end in a struggle for survival.

Reviews

An African safari might be just the ticket to get Allison Warner's life back on track. She's struggling to recover from the death of her teenage son a year ago, as her husband Burke grows increasingly distant, finding solace in his law practice.

The couple embark on an exciting safari along with a rather diverse and bizarre group of tourists; one in particular, handsome Englishman Jeremy Hoskins, makes Allison feel a way way she has no business feeling as a married woman. She throws herself recklessly into the safari, soaking in breathtaking landscapes and exotic animals...Winther certainly knows how to keep the pace moving; there's no shortage of tension as Allison and friends land in one dangerous spot after another. Winther's well-done descriptions of Africa create a lush, vibrant setting... Allison's metamorphosis from sheltered housewife to courageous woman truly centers this tale. Her desire to save her marriage, coupled with the lure of the forbidden will resonate with readers and keep them cheering for her to the novel's end. A superb thriller with enough action and suspense to keep readers well-satisfied.

Kirkus Reviews

On to Kenya! How exciting this book was, but then I knew it would be after Barbara's first book. Just being in Africa on safari has been a dream of mine and now I feel I've been there. Kenya is so beautiful and when you add to that such unusual happenings and such strange people there were, how could you not keep reading to find out how this mystery ends. Thank you, Barbara, for such an enjoyable book I could not put down and please put the next book out so I can have another fascinating adventure.

Linda J. Mahoney, world traveler

Like one of the safari vans in the story, in the hands of this gifted storyteller the plot bounces along with the frequent dips and swerves of the journey provoking revealing collisions among the widely varied group of characters. And just as on a well-planned safari, there's an exuberant profusion of wild life to observe. In fact if you read this book just before going to bed, the author's wild rendering of the sights and sounds of Kenya will insure plenty of raw material for your dreams!

Roseann M Schneider, linguist and archaeologist